Kiss Me Tomorrow

SUSAN SHREVE

 Arthur A. Levine Books

An Imprint of Scholastic Inc.

ISBN-13: 978-0-545-00150-2
ISBN-10: 0-545-00150-1

10 9 8 7 6 5 4 3 2 1   7 8 9 10 11/0

Printed in the U.S.A.   40

This edition first printing, January 2007

Book design by Elizabeth B. Parisi

To the Adorables,
ISABELA SOFIA
and
DIEGO BENJAMIN

1

Good-bye, Hello

blister was waiting for Jonah Morrison, her nose pressed against the living room window that overlooked the parking lot of the apartment where she lived with her mother and sometimes Daisy G.

Jonah was late. Eight o'clock on the first day of seventh grade at Memorial Junior High and he was already fifteen minutes late.

"Good-bye yesterday, hello tomorrow," she'd said to Jonah when they'd talked on the phone the night before and she knew by the tremor in his voice that he was nervous about junior high too.

"I don't feel any older, do you?" Jonah had asked.

"I look older, like you can tell I'm older than last year,

1

but I don't feel any different than I've always felt, if that's what you mean. Just anxious."

There was a long pause at the other end of the phone.

"Jonah? Are you still there?"

"I was thinking you do look different to me," he said. "It's a nice look."

"What does that mean?" Blister had asked.

"Just that I notice things. Nothing else."

It was a funny thing for Jonah to say, as if something in their friendship was in the process of changing, some imperceptible shift of weather that Blister sensed from Jonah but she couldn't put into words.

"So I guess it's good-bye childhood," Blister had said. "And hello . . ."

"Hello something else," Jonah had said, finishing her sentence as he sometimes did.

In the kitchen, her mother was making breakfast.

"What about a blueberry muffin?" Mary Reed called. "Or a banana?"

"I'm not hungry," Blister said, checking her reflection

in the mirror over the stained blue couch. *Too thin*, she thought. Her red hair in a high ponytail was sticking out of the back of her head like a fuzzy fat carrot. But the new plaid skirt that her grandmother, Daisy G., the dance champion of the "Seventy and Over Girls," got for her at Larson's Teens and Tweens was very sassy and so were the strappy red sandals with a tiny heel. Only the starchy white blouse her mother had ironed the night before looked juvenile, as if it belonged to a Catholic girl's school uniform, and that was not the image Blister had in mind for herself in junior high. She had put on blush, orangey-brown lipstick that matched her freckles, and her mother's mascara, which was already smudged in the corner of her pale blue eyes, but that's how the girls at Memorial Junior High came to school and Blister Reed was not about to be different yet.

"You have to have something to eat or you'll faint," her mother said, coming into the living room with a banana and a yogurt that she stuffed in the back of Blister's book bag.

"Jonah's never late. Do you think something's happened to him?" Blister asked. "Like an accident?"

"Nothing has happened to Jonah. He's probably still

at home tying his shoes or walking to our apartment in the wrong direction, his head in the clouds," Mary Reed said. "But you're going to be late for your first day of school so you better leave without him."

"I can't leave this apartment without Jonah."

Blister's stomach felt loose and watery, a funny sadness rising in her like the flu. Today, when she walked into Memorial Junior High, for the first time that she could remember, Blister Reed, the I-can-do-anything girl of the hour, *needed* Jonah Morrison at her side.

He was, after all, her best friend in the world ever since they had met in the sixth grade at Bixley Elementary. He was the new kid at school as his mother had decided to move from New York City to North Haven just after her boyfriend, Thomas Hale, left the family for good.

JONAH, THE WHALE, the sixth-graders at Bixley had written on the blackboard, referring to his size. But he didn't let their ridicule change his future at Bixley Elementary.

"Got a lemon, make lemonade," as Daisy G. would say. And Jonah tried to do just that.

"You've got to invent yourself," he had said to Blister. "That's what Thomas Hale told me and he was right. If you don't like who you are, make yourself up something better."

Jonah had made himself up as a television talk show host on his own cable network kids' show called *JONAH, THE WHALE* and had taken on Blister as his assistant.

Then in June, when school was out and the show was finished and Jonah was feeling terrible but still famous for what he had done, he told Blister the truth about himself. That after Thomas Hale, who had been like a father to him, had left his mother and him and baby Quentin to fend for themselves, Jonah had been so hungry, so completely starving to fill up his empty body, that he ate and ate and ate until he blew up like a balloon.

"You're not fat," Blister had told him. "You're normal big."

"I'm fat," Jonah had said. "I'm very fat but don't tell anyone we know."

"They can see you, Jonah. People see what's in front of them."

"Not really," he said. "They see whatever I want them to see."

Blister loved that about Jonah. He actually believed that when people looked at Jonah Morrison what they saw was his dream for himself.

"And about the lipstick," Blister's mother was saying as she headed back to the kitchen. "Wipe it off. You CANNOT wear lipstick the first day of junior high. The teachers will think you're cheap."

"What is cheap?" Blister asked, swinging her book bag over her shoulder.

"One of those bad girls you see from Memorial Junior High hanging out at the mall with a hip bone sticking out and a surly expression."

"Maybe that's just who I want to be when I go to junior high," Blister said lightly and, catching sight of Jonah Morrison rounding the corner of the parking lot, she kissed her mother, whom she loved in spite of everything, and ran down the steps two at a time.

"We're going to be late," she said.

"Everybody's late to junior high," Jonah said. "That's what Jakob Cutter said. We don't have to worry about being on time."

"Who's Jakob Cutter?" Blister asked.

"He's one of the popular guys at Memorial."

"How do you know?"

"He told me when I met him at the movies on Saturday."

"Which means he probably isn't so popular or he wouldn't have to tell you, right?"

"Wrong. You'll see." He slipped his hand in his pocket, letting one shoulder fall so his new sauntering walk gave him an attitude of confidence. "He and I are probably going to be really good friends."

"Oh yeah? You really plan ahead."

Blister felt a twinge of something. Maybe it was jealousy, she thought, although she'd never been a jealous kind of girl. Nor had she been nervous or worried or woozy. But all of a sudden, this morning, the first day of junior high, she was nervous and worried and woozy as if she might be sick. Jonah seemed different than he used to be just yesterday, when they had a smoothie at Yum Yum's, when she talked to him on the phone before she went to bed. And that set her off balance.

Jonah Morrison was almost the only person in her life she could count on completely. Jonah and Daisy G. And Blister didn't want him to change, not now, not with all the rest of the changes in her life tumbling after her like giant boulders rushing toward her, catching her unaware.

Blister knew Jonah Morrison better than anyone she had ever known. Better than she knew her mother, who could go silent for hours at a time ever since Blister's baby sister, Lila Rose, was born dead and Jack Reed had left and they'd moved from their cozy farmhouse with two old cats to an apartment where her mother cried and slept all day long. Better than she knew her father, who at forty-seven liked to think he was twenty-three years old, the same age as Tamara, who had worn a fluffy white marshmallow dress to mary Jack Reed in downtown New Haven in June in a garden and Blister wasn't even asked to be a bridesmaid. The only person she knew as well as Jonah was Daisy G., and that didn't count because Daisy

G. was exactly the same as she had been every day since Blister could remember.

"So I think my mother has a boyfriend." Blister stuck her arm through the strap of her book bag.

"Since when?"

"Since yesterday after I saw you at Yum Yum's."

"So who's your mother's boyfriend?"

"I don't know anything about him. I don't even know if he exists, only that all weekend, my last two days of vacation, my mother was locked in her bedroom whispering on the telephone to somebody she doesn't want me to know about or she wouldn't be whispering, right?"

"Who knows about women?" Jonah stopped at the light across from Memorial Junior High. "I wish my mother had a boyfriend. Then I wouldn't have to take care of Quentin all the time."

By the time the light turned, the street was full of junior high students with their book bags and low-slung pants and short, short skirts and knit caps, even though it was still hot as summer. With a sinking feeling, Blister realized that the plaid skirt and white blouse she had chosen for

9

this first day were all wrong — this significant day when every person at junior high would see her for the first time and make an assessment. The girls crowding around the stoplight were in swing skirts and see-through blouses with little camisoles or jeans with flip-flops and T-shirts.

"I'm going to feel weird here," Blister said, leaning into Jonah so the group of girls walking beside them wouldn't hear what she was saying. "What about you?"

But Jonah wasn't paying attention. He had seen someone across the street headed up the long steps at the front of the junior high and was rushing off ahead of Blister, hurrying to catch up.

"Wait for me," Blister said, and immediately she was sorry she had said anything, sorry to need Jonah Morrison to be with her on this first day of junior high. She didn't *want* to need anyone, had never needed anyone before, not since her parents separated and she started a new life as Blister Reed. And she wasn't about to change now.

Mary Reed called Blister Alyssa, which was her real name. But the year the Reeds moved from the country to the apartment in North Haven, the year Lila Rose was born dead and her father went off with Tamara and her mother got lost in a jumble of sadness in her own head, she had changed her name from Alyssa to Blister.

"Blister is what happens when your shoes are too tight," she had explained when she went to Bixley Elementary, her new school in North Haven.

In her head, Blister had become the girl she was — red-haired, pink-cheeked with a splash of fawn freckles, skinny as a straw, with a roller-coaster brain that zipped through the day on high speed.

"That's Jakob Cutter," Jonah called over his shoulder to Blister as he hurried up the steps. "The guy I told you about." He hurried to catch up to Jakob Cutter, who was walking with a group of boys in low-slung jeans and over-size long shirts and high-tops.

"Hey Jakob," Jonah called, but Jakob didn't look back. Instead he slung his arm around the shoulder of a smaller, skinny black-haired boy and together they walked in the front door of Memorial Junior High.

"I guess he was in a hurry," Jonah said as Blister caught up with him.

"I guess he was."

"Maybe I'll do something with him after school." Jonah got in the line with Blister for locker and home-room assignments. "Go to the mall or something. I'll let you know."

"Never mind," Blister said coolly. "I have plans after school."

Which wasn't exactly true. Her plan was the same as it had always been all last year at Bixley Elementary, all summer, ever since she met Jonah. Either they'd be at her apartment or Jonah's apartment, depending on the day.

But maybe those sweet afternoons with Jonah were about to be over.

2
Preview of Coming Attractions

blister wasn't exactly unhappy in seventh grade at Memorial Junior High. It wasn't in her nature to *be* unhappy, as she told Daisy G. at the end of the first week of school in September. But she had troubles.

"Everyone has troubles in seventh grade," Daisy G. had said.

"Not troubles like what's happening with Jonah."

"Like what?"

"Like our friendship is dying. Just drying up and disappearing."

Daisy G. was lying on Blister's bed next to Blister, her head propped up on the pillow doing her leg exercises, pointing her toes so they curled under in tight little balls.

"I don't think so, buttercup. Not with Jonah Morrison."

"But on our first day at Memorial," Blister began, "Jonah was supposed to meet me and come to my apartment and instead he followed this stupid bull of a boy called Monster Bar to the drugstore, trailing behind him like a lost puppy, and when I called him he didn't even turn around. And then on Tuesday he picked me up as usual, but at the stoplight at the avenue near school, he saw this other freaky guy called Jakob Cutter and nearly got killed crossing the street against the light to catch up with him. And on Wednesday, he didn't pick me up at all even though he'd promised. 'Wait for me at the edge of your parking lot,' he said and I waited and he didn't come."

"Forget him. Men like that are not worth a penny of your time."

"But these boys he's so in love with don't even like him."

"He'll have to find that out for himself."

"He's not a quick learner, you know."

"He'll learn if you make your own friends."

"I am making new friends," Blister said. She had

walked home with a girl named Eva and stopped at Engel's Coffee Shop with some of her old friends from Bixley, and the girl who sat in the next desk in English literature had asked her to her birthday party. But it wasn't the same.

"Also, I met Frank Holt today and I didn't even know he existed and I think I hate him."

"You hardly know him yet and we need to give him a chance," Daisy G. replied, reaching her knobby arms above her head in a semicircle, her feet in the air in second position. "He could turn out to be no trouble at all."

"I know him well enough already to wish he'd evaporate."

Frank Holt arrived at the Reeds' apartment that Sunday morning after the first week of school while Blister's mother was at the drugstore picking up hydrogen peroxide and milk. Blister was lying on the couch in the living room, staring out the window thinking about seventh grade, wondering what her life would be like in junior high without Jonah and, now that she'd been in school for a week, how she should dress for it. She imagined herself wearing a short red swing skirt and a black turtleneck, maybe matching red lipstick. Just as she was about to get up to try on her mother's plum-red lipstick, Frank Holt ran up the steps to the Reeds' apartment singing, *"Mary, Mary, quite contrary, How does your garden grow?"*

It was too hot to breathe in North Haven, Connecticut. The air conditioner in the living room window was broken, the air too still to move, and Blister's face was wet with perspiration. She wiped her arm across her damp cheeks and turned the doorknob.

Frank Holt was standing in the hall wearing a white T-shirt with *Grane's Landscaping* written in green, and khaki shorts with a stripe of dirt across the front, his large arms full of yellow roses.

"Hello, hello," he said. "You must be Alyssa. I was singing a song for your mother." And he started up again with *"Mary, Mary, quite contrary, How does your garden grow? With silver bells and cockle shells and pretty maids in a row."*

"My mother isn't here."

"She's not here? She told me she'd be here all morning."

16

He stepped just inside the front door.

"She's getting things at the drugstore."

"She said she would be here and I was to meet her at exactly now and we were going to take you to lunch."

Blister rocked back on her heels, her heart pounding in her chest, her knees weak. As far as she knew, her mother didn't have any friends in North Haven except the ones at the flower shop. All of her friends were the old friends she had made when she and Jack Reed and Blister had lived in the country. How could she have a man in her life who knew her well enough to bring flowers on a Sunday morning, unless the whispers on the telephone calls she'd been having in the last week, hidden away in her bedroom, were with this man who sang nursery rhymes in public places?

"Who are you?" Blister folded her arms across her chest.

"You don't *know* who I am?"

His hand holding the flowers dropped down so the roses touched the ground, and Blister could tell he was genuinely surprised.

"I've never heard of you before." Her voice was thin.

"I'm Frank Holt."

"I don't know a Frank Holt," Blister said, folding her arms across her chest, conscious that she wasn't smiling, that her eyes were narrow and her lips trembling. But she was beginning to understand that her mother *did* know him, *must* know him, or he wouldn't have come up the steps to their apartment with such enthusiastic expectation.

He was large and burly with a big head of black, curly hair and a broad chest and large hands that at the moment were wrapped around the yellow roses like sewer pipes.

"I work with your mother," he said quietly.

For the last two years since Jack Reed had left to live with Tamara, Mary Reed had been very unhappy. Sometimes she sat for hours on the couch in the living room staring into space. Or called in sick to the flower shop where she worked and stayed in bed all day until afternoon, when Blister came home from elementary school.

"You work at the flower shop?"

"In landscaping."

"So are you her boyfriend?"

Boyfriend. Her mother couldn't have a boyfriend. She didn't need one. She had Blister and Daisy G. and even though she used to be married to Jack Reed, that didn't mean she had to replace him with a stranger. Blister took in puffs of air, trying to breathe deep in her chest so she wouldn't faint.

"My mother will be back soon," Blister said, and she stepped back so Frank Holt could walk all the way inside the apartment.

"Good. I'll wait for her in the living room."

"That's fine," Blister said. "Have a seat, and when she comes, tell her I've left."

"But we were taking you to lunch."

"My mother didn't tell me about lunch and I have other plans."

Blister picked up her wallet, stuck the key to the front door in the pocket of her shorts, and walked past Frank. She headed down the steps and out the door of the apartment complex on her way to Jonah Morrison's apartment, seven blocks north and two blocks west from hers.

Blister was not in the habit of talking about her

personal problems the way other girls, especially in the sixth grade, had done, complaining about their mothers and their fathers and the teachers at Bixley Elementary.

"Stiff upper lip," Daisy G. would say. "Smile and the world smiles with you. Cry and you cry alone."

Blister didn't cry at all, not since first grade that she could remember. But sometimes when things with Mary Reed were difficult and the empty apartment had gotten too lonely, she would complain to Jonah. He was the only one outside her family who knew that her daily life wasn't all sunshine. She had told him about her father and Tamara and about Lila Rose, and Jonah had told her everything that had happened to him, good and bad, whether it was true or not.

With the unexpected arrival of Frank Holt at her apartment, Blister desperately needed to talk to Jonah Morrison. She forgave him all of his omissions and unkindness to her as she hurried to his building, imagining what would happen when she got there. Of course he wanted to be accepted at junior high. Of course he wanted to be one of the popular boys and even though his choice of friends, like Monster Bar and Jakob Cutter, was foolish and would bring him bad luck, Blister understood, and at this moment she needed to talk to him enough to forgive him for letting her down.

The noon sun was blazing overhead, the streets empty of cars, and by the time Blister arrived at Jonah's apartment, walked up the steps, and knocked on the door, her T-shirt was soaking wet with perspiration. Ms. Morrison would have lemonade, Blister was thinking, and they'd drink it in Jonah's room with the air conditioner humming, lying on the floor, their feet propped up on Jonah's bed while Blister told him the bad news about Frank Holt.

But Jonah wasn't home.

So she walked from his apartment, north on Frederick Street, across Frederick Park where an old man was sleeping in the heat on a park bench with his skinny cat lying underneath the bench, a leash around its neck.

The old man opened his eyes and said, "Do you have any spare change?" Blister hurried past him to the other side of the park and Blake Street where the shops were, walking slowly along Blake Street, stopping to look in the windows of the ice cream store, and Teens and

Tots Clothing, and the pet store where a gray-and-black shaggy mutt wildly wagged his skinny tail when she looked in at him. She crossed at Barron Street and up the back way to Bixley Elementary where she used to go to school. Just last June she'd graduated in a white dotted-Swiss dress and little high heels and, to her great surprise, won first prize for Best Personality.

Andy Sorrow sat on the front steps of Bixley, looking as if he'd been crying all morning, his face bright red and swollen and wet.

Blister crouched beside him.

Andy was a few grades behind her and she didn't know him well, only that he had a reputation as a wimp and a whiner and a baby and the older boys teased him.

"My mother's in England," he said, tears running down his cheek. "She's on a trip and I hate the babysitter."

"How come?"

"She says I'm invading her space with my unhappiness."

Blister rested her chin in her hands.

"So I ran away from home," he said.

"Me too. I ran away from home this morning."

"Why did you run away?"

"Just because there're too many people in my apartment."

Blister wasn't going to tell Andy Sorrow about Frank Holt. She hardly knew Andy but she was glad to find him on the steps, even glad that he was having a bad day. Just sitting beside him made her feel better.

"I'm hoping the babysitter will call my mother when I don't come back and my mother will come home from England to find me."

"I hope that happens," Blister said.

"I hope the people you don't like in your apartment go away."

Andy Sorrow reached into his pocket and took out a red lollipop wrapped in cellophane.

"Want this?" he asked.

"Thank you very much," Blister said, getting up, removing the cellophane from the lollipop, and sticking it in her mouth. "A lollipop is exactly what I want."

And she walked down the street toward her apartment feeling much better, feeling almost well.

*　　*　　*

That night, Blister waited until she heard her mother hang up the telephone and go into her bedroom, and then she climbed out of her bed, pushed open the door to her mother's room, and turned on the overhead light.

"You didn't tell me you had a boyfriend."

"I thought you'd be pleased, Alyssa. I've been so gloomy and it upsets you to see me gloomy, so I thought you'd want me to have a new friend."

"I don't want you to have a boyfriend who arrives at the house with flowers before I've even heard that he exists."

"We had planned to take you to lunch and tell you then."

"You're my mother," Blister said, leaning against the door. "You should have told me first, before lunch. You should have asked me if I *wanted* to go to lunch before what's-his-name, the *boyfriend*, knocked on the front door with his bad surprise."

"I'm sorry, Alyssa." Mary Reed was sitting on the edge of the bed in her nightgown. "Frank works at the flower shop and we've been good friends ever since I started to work there. We know each other very well."

"But I don't know him and I'm your daughter."

"I didn't want you to know about him until I was sure it was going to work out between us."

"What do you mean, *work out*?" Blister asked.

"You know. Be together."

"Like Dad and Tamara?"

Mary Reed started to reply but Blister had already turned away, shut the bedroom door, and headed into her own room, sitting down on the edge of the bed in the middle of the outfits she'd been trying on for junior high. From the bed, she could see herself in the full-length mirror on her closet door.

At night, red lipstick looked better on a redhead. It was too bright to wear in the daytime. Maybe she'd wear pale pink lip gloss for the second week of school at Memorial Junior High and one of the hand-me-down skirts from Tamara, probably the grass-green one with lace on the hem, and her frizzy red hair in a high ponytail. Maybe mascara.

Sometimes, Blister was thinking, the only person in the world she could really count on was herself, and that was not enough.

3

The Beginning of the Story

blister read about Jonah Morrison as she sat up in bed with the *New Haven Morning News* resting on her knees.

It was early October, the beginning of cold weather in North Haven, Connecticut, and a night chill had frosted the windows of her bedroom silvery white. The sun rising over the town lit the red leaves of the oak tree outside and a rainbow of golden red shimmered across the glass.

Blister was checking the newspaper for local murders, something she liked to do on Saturday mornings since murders, if they happened, usually took place in downtown New Haven on a Friday night.

She got her interest in murders from Daisy G., who

kept a stack of murder mysteries beside her bed. At breakfast, when Blister had a sleepover, Daisy G. would tell murder stories as if she'd been a witness to each one. Blister listened to Daisy G.'s stories but she preferred the ones in the newspaper, the real ones. They gave an edge of danger to her life in the almost-city of North Haven.

On this first Saturday in October there were no murders reported, only a gunfight on Anderson Avenue with minor injuries, a bar fire at Olsson's that sent one customer to the emergency room, and a hit-and-run accident on the parkway in which an elderly woman broke her hip.

The story that captured Blister's attention was in the Metro section, second page.

Student Shoplifting, the story began. "A Memorial Junior High School student was taken into custody for shoplifting Friday evening at the midtown bus station."

Blister *knew* in her heart that the student taken into custody for shoplifting was Jonah Morrison.

It was just an instinct, but that's the way Blister Reed came to conclusions. She was like a terrier-mix mutt from the pound, as Daisy G. would say. *All* instinct. Razor-sharp eyes, electric ears, and an excellent sniffer.

There was no suggestion in the newspaper story that the student was Jonah Morrison, no personal details, and the student's name couldn't be released to the press because of his age. But there was something in the description of "an adolescent boy found loitering in front of the bus station and arrested after police discovered a stash of electronic equipment in his backpack shoplifted from Ram's Electronics, located adjacent to the bus station."

Blister could see Jonah in her mind's eye. He would have been hanging out at the bus station where the kids from this part of town went on the weekends, an uninvited guest, leaning against the worn brick building in a casual sort of way, an expression of boredom on his face, imitating the other boys at Memorial Junior High, his hands in his pockets, his eyes half-closed, longing to be popular.

Jonah was always longing to be popular or famous or important and he had worked hard at it. He and Blister had tried to be famous together with their television talk show on local cable and for a while it even worked and they were famous. Especially Jonah. But that didn't last.

Lately, since the second week of school, whenever Blister saw Jonah in the halls or behind the school or walking into town, he was alone or almost alone, always outside the group of popular boys, just behind them, out of breath, hurrying to keep up.

As Blister imagined the scene at the bus station, the police had arrived after a call about missing merchandise from Ram's Electronics. They hopped out of the patrol car and, sweeping the streets for loiterers, they discovered Jonah standing with his backpack, a look of confusion or bewilderment on his face, not quick enough to understand what was going on.

The boys, professional troublemakers from Memorial Junior High whom Jonah had followed to the bus station, probably had stuffed their own stash of stolen electronic goods in Jonah Morrison's backpack and bolted without a trace, leaving Jonah to take the consequences alone.

Jonah should have known himself better. He was a daydreamer, lost in his own invented world, and he needed Blister Reed, who always knew exactly what was going on around her because she paid attention to details. But since school started, Jonah wanted nothing to do with his former best friend, so it was no wonder he had gotten into trouble.

"But I didn't shoplift," Jonah would have said to the police. "I don't know how this stuff got in my backpack."

It wasn't in his character to steal.

"We don't know the guy," the other boys from Memorial Junior High would have said of Jonah if the police had caught them. "He goes to our school but he's not in our group," they'd say.

Which was the kind of cocky, sullen-faced, mean-acting boys they were.

"They're my friends," Jonah had said to Blister when they had lunch that week in the cafeteria.

"You wish," Blister said crossly. "They aren't worth your time."

But there was no telling Jonah anything. He believed what he wanted to believe whether it was true or not.

Blister got out of bed, folded the newspaper into a square, slipped on her jeans, and climbed on her desk to survey the mess in her bedroom. She was supposed to be packing and cleaning and filling the green garbage bags with the collection of junk she'd accumulated over the

30

two years she had lived with her mother in this apartment.

Today they were moving to a fancier part of town. She'd still be in the seventh grade at Memorial Junior High, but she'd be living on the edge of the rich section of the Memorial district with her mother and Frank Holt, instead of the edge of the poor section with her mother and occasionally Daisy G.

In the living room, her mother was arguing with Daisy G. about giving the Salvation Army the rocking chair that had been a gift from her ex-husband, Jack Reed, when Blister was born.

"It's a perfectly good rocking chair," Daisy G. was saying. "And why should it remind you of Jack Reed when it's where you rocked your darling angel daughter?"

"She's not my angel," her mother said.

Blister put her hands over her ears.

Her mother drove her crazy. Ever since the divorce, her mother's mood became a barometer for stormy weather. Blister tiptoed in and out of favor several times a day, sometimes the worst daughter any mother ever had, sometimes the best. She could never predict.

"Just wait!" Daisy G. had said to Blister. "Menopause. Your mother's in men-o-pause," as if Blister didn't know the meaning of the word. "Be patient. It'll be over soon."

"Not soon enough," Blister replied.

"Trust me! It even happened to me when I was your mother's age."

But Blister couldn't remember a time when Daisy G. hadn't been the same sparkling little woman, buzzing through life like a hummingbird, gathering the sweetest nectar wherever she poked her beak.

The living room was full of boxes packed to move to the new house on Acorn Street, which had a garden, a wraparound front porch, a bedroom in the refinished attic for Blister, and the addition of Frank Holt, who was at least an improvement over her father's girlfriend, now wife, with her tiny bottom and sickly sweet French perfume and bad temper whenever Blister was around.

"We don't have enough furniture for a house," Blister said, slipping the newspaper under her arm and opening the door to her bedroom. "So keep the rocker."

"My point exactly!"

Daisy G. was holding on to the rocker, dressed in her leotard as she was every morning, doing her ballet exercises on bare knobby feet, white as snow. All her life, Daisy G. had been a dancer, and now at seventy-five, she was the blue-ribbon dance champion in the "Seventy and Over" category. She was small and thin with tiny hands and tiny feet and frizzy hair that she'd recently started to dye the color of golden peaches.

"I want new furniture for my new life," her mother said.

"Have whatever your heart desires, sweetheart."

Daisy G. checked out her form in the mirror over the couch, raising her arm in a half-moon over her head.

"That's my motto. We only have one round-trip ticket on this planet."

"Round-trip?" Blister asked, slipping into the rocker.

"One life. Birth to death. Dust to dust. Dead is dead," Daisy G. said cheerfully. "Don't miss your chance to hop aboard the happiness train."

Her mother shrugged.

"And what does your heart desire, Alyssa?" Daisy G. asked.

"Maybe I'll be Alyssa when I'm older and fall in love with some great-looking hunk in high school," she said. "But I'm just myself for now."

"Don't fall in love soon," her mother said. "I was too young to have any sense when I met your father."

"Love is good," Daisy G. contradicted. "I'm always in love. Right now I'm in love with young Eddie at the pharmacy who gives me my heart pills, but I was mad for Will Swindells when I was in the second grade." She stretched her hamstrings, leaning over to touch her toes. Then, straightening her back and turning out her toes, she stood in first position. "It didn't work out between Will and me, but who cares? He gave me a milk chocolate Hershey bar for Easter and that was a chocolate bar I wouldn't have had without Will Swindells."

Blister was not in love. Not now, not ever, and she didn't plan to change anytime soon.

Jonah Morrison was the only boy she had ever loved and that was a different kind of love. He had never been a boyfriend. In spite of all the other girls who giggled and squealed in the girls' room about Jakob Cutter or Monster Bar or Spunk or Eddie James or the cutest or the hunkiest or this boy or that boy — Blister was too busy with other plans to worry about boyfriends.

"So listen to what I read this morning in the newspaper," she said, opening the paper and reading the column about shoplifting. "Who does that sound like to you guys?"

"Like every boy at Memorial Junior High or any other place in town with teenage boys," her mother said, piling her long hair on top of her head and fastening it with a barrette. "Why do you ask?"

"Daisy G.?"

"You're going to say Jonah Morrison, aren't you?" Daisy G. collapsed on the couch, her dancing feet resting on the arm of it.

"That's what I thought when I read the story," Blister said. "I don't think he shoplifted, but it would be just like Jonah to be caught with the goods."

"Because he's the only one you know stupid enough to be caught." Daisy G. shook her head.

"Innocent enough."

"Foolish enough," Daisy G. continued, enjoying herself this morning.

Mary Reed went into her bedroom and closed the door.

"You know what I wish," Daisy G. said to Blister. "If I could take Jonah Morrison for hot chocolate and cheesecake at the coffeehouse one afternoon, I'd teach him how to walk straight through his teenage years into his tomorrow." She sat up on her elbow, her lips drawn in a red line straight across the bottom of her face. "In his tomorrow, a boy like Jonah could be someone amazing."

"I know that, Daisy G.," Blister said.

"Just one afternoon with me is all it would take," she said. "I'd give him my You're-the-Best class and he'd be a different boy."

Blister shook her head.

"I don't think so, Daisy G." She got up from the rocker. "The only thing Jonah wants is to belong to the popular group. Cheesecake is no competition."

Blister picked up the newspaper with the story about Jonah, or *maybe* Jonah, and slapped barefoot into her bedroom to finish packing.

"Frank is coming soon," her mother called just before

she shut the bedroom door. "He's bringing the truck, so I hope you're almost ready."

"Ready enough," Blister replied, and even she could hear the melancholy in the tone of her voice.

Blister was in the fourth grade when her mother had been pregnant with Lila Rose. She was an only child, tired of being alone, tired of all the attention from her mother and father and Daisy G., so much she sometimes felt she could drown in it.

All that winter, she thought about the baby every day — what they would do together, what she would teach her. And then something happened to Lila Rose and she was dead before she even got to be born.

"Bad things happen," Daisy G. told her crisply. "That's life and we make the most of it."

Which Blister had done even when her family fell apart, even when her mother went to bed for days at a time, too sad to cook dinner. And when her father married Tamara.

"Mettle, that's what you've got," Daisy G. had told her.

"Metal?" Blister had asked.

"Mettle is what you're made of. Metal with heart and a sense of humor."

And now Frank Holt had come along, upsetting Blister's life as she knew it, stealing her mother from her so that nothing was left she could count on in her family but Daisy G.

"Are you ready?" Her mother knocked on her door. "Alyssa, do you hear me?"

"I'd have to be unconscious not to hear you," Blister said, but quietly. Whatever she thought of Frank Holt, she didn't want to disturb her mother's happiness.

When Mary Reed opened the door, Blister was sitting on her bed rereading the piece about shoplifting in the morning paper.

"Oh, Alyssa, you don't even know that the boy in that story is Jonah."

"Yes, I do," Blister said. "It has to be Jonah."

4
Gone for Good

When the telephone rang, Daisy G. was packing up the dishes in the kitchen and Blister was in her bedroom painting her nails lime green for the move to Acorn Street.

"The phone's for you." Mary Reed, in her bathrobe with a towel around her head, leaned into Blister's room. "It's Jonah's mother. She wants to speak to you."

Blister took a deep breath, sliding down the wall until she was sitting on her haunches, the phone pressed against her ear.

"I got news for you, Blister Reed," Jonah's mother said, her voice strong and just the slightest bit angry.

*   *   *

Jonah's mother was tough — the way she spoke without a hint of worry in her voice, the way she stood, squared off, her arms folded across her chest like weapons, the expression on her face fixed for combat. And she had reasons. No money, for one. She had two boys — Jonah and baby Quentin — and two jobs, one in the cafeteria at a junior high in New Haven and the other driving a city bus in a wide loop around North Haven for the early-morning and late-evening shifts. And she had a shiftless boyfriend, Thomas Hale, who came in and out of her life like a magazine salesman, taking her money and forgetting to deliver the magazines. If it weren't for Aunt Lavinia, Jonah's aunt who took the boys in while his mother drove the late shift, Jonah would be raising himself.

"Jonah's gone for good," Ms. Morrison said. "That's what the note he left me on the kitchen table this morning said. *'Gone for good, Mama, and I am sorry for breaking your heart.'*"

Blister took the portable phone from her bedroom to the bathroom so her mother didn't overhear her conversation.

"Don't get me wrong. Jonah didn't break my heart," Ms. Morrison said. "My heart's made out of iron and there's no breaking it."

There wasn't a slip of sadness in her voice, not a crack or shimmer of tears, but Blister knew better. She had watched Ms. Morrison on Saturday afternoons cooking up a storm so her boys would have hot dinners all week, ruffling Jonah's hair, listening to his wild stories about his successes and all the good and popular friends he pretended to have.

If it was true that Jonah had gone for good, Ms. Morrison's heart would break in pieces and nobody, not even her former boyfriend Thomas Hale, could fix it.

"Do you know what happened?" Blister asked.

"I know he followed Jakob Cutter and Monster Bar and some of the other criminals in the seventh grade down to the bus station and somehow he got caught with electronic equipment in his backpack and the criminals bolted and Jonah made the morning paper for shoplifting."

"I read that."

"And you knew the student was Jonah, didn't you?" She gave a dry laugh. "Who else in junior high would be standing in the middle of the sidewalk paying no attention to what was going on around him and get caught for doing something he didn't do? I raised a fool for a son and it's costing me."

In the background, baby Quentin was crying for a chocolate cookie.

Jonah's mother was the mother Blister wanted to be if she ever got far enough along in life to be one. Straight-talking and funny and hard on kids but fair. Always she was fair. She didn't go silent or moan about her troubles the way Blister's mom could do, even though Ms. Morrison had plenty of troubles. She wasn't mushy or sentimental or even sweet about her sons.

Anyone who saw Ms. Morrison with her boys, as Blister had every Saturday for months, knew they were her golden treasures, her "precious little fools" as she called them, rubbing her chin in their thick curly hair.

But this morning, Blister could feel the heat of Ms. Morrison's anger through the telephone wires.

"Do you know this boy Jakob Cutter?" she was saying. "He's the leader of the group of criminals Jonah has

42

fallen in love with and he's older than the rest of them and so dumb, he's actually smart."

Blister didn't *know* Jakob Cutter, but of course she'd seen him all the time, rushing away from Jonah with his gang. He was tall and thin, with a fuzzy beard like a cotton ball at the bottom of his chin. *Hot*, according to the conversation she had overheard in the girls' locker room. *Mean as a snake*, according to Blister, who had an instinct for *mean* and stayed way clear of boys like Jakob.

"Jakob Cutter could kill a person dead with those cold blue eyes and curly lips of his," Ms. Morrison was saying. "Jonah didn't shoplift. It's not in his character."

"I know he didn't," Blister said.

"He isn't the kind of boy who can face a problem straight on. He'd rather sink into the ground and disappear," Ms. Morrison said. "So I'm going to need all the help I can get."

"I'll do everything I can," Blister said.

After she hung up the phone, Blister sat very still, looking at the bare white wall, a gnawing hunger in her stomach as if she hadn't eaten for weeks. She had not promised Ms. Morrison anything. She'd agreed that what happened to Jonah was unfair and boys like Monster Bar and Eddie James were dreadful boys on their way to being criminals and Jakob Cutter was the worst of all.

Blister didn't say that she would try to find Jonah, although of course she would.

Soon. Today. Before she packed another box.

She reached up and turned the lock on the bathroom door so she could think about what she was going to do. Just thinking about Jonah somewhere dark and hidden, scared to death, his small, black eyes darting like fireflies, broke Blister's heart in spite of how angry and hurt she had been. He was a sweet and funny boy, only thirteen years old and in some ways already full-grown, filled out like a man, with the soul of an innocent baby. He didn't recognize bad news when he saw it walking down the street.

"The only defense that boy has is his imagination," Daisy G. had said to Blister last year after Jonah's television show closed. "He couldn't hurt a flea. He doesn't have it in him."

And Daisy G. was right.

When trouble came, what Jonah did was pretend he was someone else, someone grand or famous or important, someone with a big future ahead of him.

Right now, wherever he was hiding out behind closed doors, Blister was sure he was planning a miracle.

Frank Holt was standing in the middle of the living room in cowboy boots and Levi's, his square-cut beard sticking out like porcupine quills. Slung over his shoulder as usual was Bewilder, an old, yellow, bad-smelling tabby cat with missing clumps of hair along its back.

"So, Missy Alyssy, how's tricks?" he asked as Blister walked into the room, collapsing on the couch.

She didn't reply. She never replied to his silly jokes.

"Be of good faith, Alyssa," Frank was saying. "This is our reincarnation day and I'm taking you from poor to almost rich in a matter of hours. We'll have a splendid new life, you and your mom and me."

Blister actually wanted to like Frank Holt because he made her mother happier than she had been for a very long time. Even Daisy G., who had her reservations about Frank, believed he had rescued Mary Reed from a long misery when no one else could do it. Not even Blister.

But Frank wasn't an easy man to like. He filled the apartment with his large personality, warm and high-spirited and full of stories. He was too noisy, though, and Blister didn't like the way he talked.

Missy Alyssy. Funny Oney. Girly Squirrelly. Daisy Waisy. And then he'd laugh out loud as if he thought he was some kind of comic genius.

She wished he'd get rid of the smelly cat and cut his beard and call her Blister. She wished he wasn't so cheerful and sure of himself and self-congratulatory, believing he had arrived in the Reeds' life in the nick of time.

"Things were fine until he came," Blister said to Daisy G.

"Not exactly fine, Alyssa," Daisy G. said. "Your mother was depressed and Frank put an end to that."

And Blister was grateful that her mother dressed up when Frank was around and put on lipstick and curled her hair and didn't lie around in bed any longer like she used to do, waiting for the afternoon soap operas or for night to come. She just wished she didn't have to live on the top floor of their new house with her mother and Frank cooing at each other on the floor below.

"Bad news about Jonah?" Daisy G. asked, sitting on the couch next to Blister, running her fingers through her hair.

"I was right about the story in the paper today."

"Poor Jonah. He's just an accident waiting to happen."

"And now he's gone," Blister said.

"Gone?" Daisy G. asked. "What does that mean?"

"He left a note for Ms. Morrison to say he was gone for good."

Daisy G. pressed Blister's hand between her knurly fingers.

"Then we'll have to find him, pronto, before it gets too dark tonight."

"That's what I'm planning to do."

"And you will," Daisy G. said. "You're a *can-do, look at-the-bright-side* kind of girl."

Mary Reed's bedroom door opened and she slapped her bare feet across the hardwood floor, the sweet smell of her new gardenia perfume floating across the room to the couch where Blister was sitting.

"Good morning, Wary Mary," Frank said, slipping Bewilder off his shoulder and kissing the top of Mary's head.

"Not wary, Frank. Not wary any longer," Mary Reed said with a girlish laugh.

"So today's the day we move to Paradise," he said.

"Paradise?" Blister asked, her knees drawn up under her chin, pressing against Daisy G., who gave her a little pinch on the elbow, whispering a warm breathy *hush* in her ear.

"I'm almost packed," Mary Reed said. "If you'll take these boxes to the truck, darling." She pointed to a stack of boxes by the front door. "Then Alyssa can go with you to see the new house and I'll finish up boxing the books in the living room and Daisy G. will do the kitchen."

"I have already *seen* the new house," Blister said.

"Not in the daytime," her mother said.

"There was light enough to see what I needed to see," Blister said. "It's a perfectly nice house."

"Maybe you'll *help* Frank move in then anyway," Mary

Reed said, giving Blister one of her that-will-be-enough looks.

"I can't help. I have responsibilities to Jonah today," Blister said.

But Mary Reed wasn't listening. She had wandered over to the large apartment window overlooking the parking lot and watched Frank load the boxes on the truck.

Blister slipped past her mother and followed Daisy G. to the kitchen.

"I hate his cat."

"It's not the cat that's bothering you, sweet pea. The cat is just a cat."

Daisy G. pulled out a kitchen drawer halfway to her waist and lifted her leg, resting it there, reaching to touch her toes.

"It's not easy being a girl moving into a house with an old clown and his old cat."

"Not easy, but you're a chin-up, feisty girl, so put a good face on it, look ahead, the future is brighter, tomorrow is another day." Daisy G. kissed the top of Blister's head. "Besides, you have to find Jonah, yes?"

"I do."

"So forget Frank. He's your mama's mashed potato, not yours." Daisy G. put a bony arm around Blister's shoulders and pulled her close. "You've got your own happily ever after to think about."

Blister put her cheek against Daisy G.'s painted, powdery face.

"Where would you go if you were Jonah?" she asked.

"I don't know where but I know I'd go by train."

"Maybe he'd go to New York where he used to live," Blister said.

"If I were Jonah, I'd go west. Wyoming. Colorado. High mountain places."

"Or Boston where Thomas Hale lives."

"Or he could be right under our noses," Daisy G. said. "You'll find him. You have the best sniffer I know."

5

An Unexpected Coincidence

blister sat in the cab of Frank Holt's Chevrolet pickup truck, her feet resting on an old battery, the window down, a light rain misting her face.

Beside her, Frank was tapping on the steering wheel. His hands and feet were always moving, tap-tap-tapping as if the music was playing in his head.

"Alyssa?" His voice was tentative.

"Could you call me Blister?" she replied. "I like to be called by my present name."

They were on their way to Jonah Morrison's brown-brick apartment complex in Springfield, the development next to where Blister lived. Frank had agreed to stop first at the Morrisons', where the police were taking down some missing-person information, or at least that's what

Ms. Morrison had thought when she called Blister a second time, asking her to get herself over to Jonah's apartment pronto.

"So tell me about Jonah," Frank asked.

"He's sort of my best friend, at least he was, and he's disappeared."

Blister was watching the houses whip past her window, her head turned away from Frank Holt so she didn't have to look at his scruffy face or the way his belly folded over his belt or the little brown circle on the side of his face with a black hair coming out the middle of it.

"Best friend or boyfriend?"

Frank turned in to the apartment complex where Jonah lived, searching for a place to park his truck.

"I didn't say boyfriend." She unlocked the door, ready to get out. "I don't have a boyfriend."

Blister had considered Jonah. Lying in her bed at night under a bright sky, unable to sleep for all the thoughts flying through her head, she'd imagined kissing Jonah Morrison. Just for a moment, she'd pictured the two of them in the dark together in her room where they used to talk and talk all Saturday afternoon into evening.

In her daydream, Jonah would lean over to kiss her lips.

"Kiss me tomorrow," she'd say to him, pleased that he wanted to kiss her and a little frightened.

And then she'd fall asleep.

When she woke up in the morning, everything would have changed with sunlight pouring through her window. By day, it was impossible for Blister to imagine kissing Jonah Morrison ever.

"About time for a boyfriend, isn't it? Seventh grade. I had a girlfriend in seventh grade called Melissa. She had dark curly hair and blue eyes and a dimple on her chin. I can't remember her last name."

Blister fell silent. She didn't like the way Frank Holt insinuated himself into her life, laying a claim on her. But she had to admit, she was flattered by his interest.

And sad too because her own father never showed the kind of interest in Blister's life that Frank did.

He turned the truck into a parking space across from the Morrisons' apartment.

"Go ahead into the apartment and I'll listen to the radio until you get back," he said.

"I'll hurry," Blister said, jumping out of the cab.

"Don't worry," he said. "Take your time."

Upstairs in Jonah's small, cheerful apartment with yellow walls and red couches, Ms. Morrison brought in lemonade and a plate of sweet rolls, carrying Quentin on her hip.

Blister sat on the edge of a hard-back chair, and Ms. Morrison sat on the couch across from her.

"I'm trying to figure things out," Ms. Morrison began. "Jonah's changed since you two were best friends at Bixley. I don't like it and I don't know what to make of it."

Quentin climbed off his mother's lap, sat down at Blister's feet, and untied her tennis shoes, putting the ends of the laces in his mouth.

"He's making new friends now," Blister said. "Only once since school started did we walk home together like we used to do and stop to get a smoothie at Yum Yum's and talk about his plans to be famous."

"And now what happens?"

"That was almost three weeks ago and now he's made other friends and I almost never see him except sometimes at lunch."

"Did he ever talk about Thomas Hale?" Ms. Morrison asked.

"He did. Last year he talked about Thomas a lot."

"It's a shame. A boy needs a father." She took the shoelace out of Quentin's mouth and put him on her lap. "I've filed a missing-child report with the police and they want to know the facts about Jonah's daily life so they'll have a better chance at finding him."

"I used to know everything about his daily life but I don't any longer. Not since he started following these popular guys at Memorial and hanging out at the bus station."

"They're the wrong friends for Jonah."

"I think he wants to be cool and popular."

"Well, it's not going to happen. He's got the wrong blood for popular. But I don't think he shoplifted."

"He wouldn't know how to do it," Blister said.

"That's the truth, but we can't ever really know what another person is capable of doing," Ms. Morrison said. "And I should know everything about Jonah because he's my son."

"I think I used to know everything about Jonah," Blister said, finishing the sweet roll and tying the wet laces of her sneakers. "And maybe that old Jonah is still there."

"I hope you're right," Ms. Morrison said.

Blister thought she heard tears in her voice, but she couldn't be sure. Ms. Morrison was a strong woman.

Frank Holt had fallen asleep. He looked older sleeping than he did when he was awake, his skin loose under his chin, his eyes sagging. Blister tapped him on the arm.

"So how was that?"

"Weird to be there with Jonah gone," Blister said. "Ms. Morrison made lemonade and sweet rolls and I thought I had to eat them and then we sat in their living room and she asked questions about Jonah and me so she could tell the police for their missing-child report."

"And she hasn't a clue about what's happened?"

"Not so far." Blister drew her knees up under her chin. "I'm thinking I'll be able to imagine where he is now. Sometimes I can do that."

"He was probably scared to death when he got caught at the bus station," Frank said.

"I know he was. And completely confused when the police discovered the electronic equipment in his backpack."

"So you're pretty sure he didn't shoplift?"

Blister nodded.

"It'd be pretty hard to get electronic equipment into someone's backpack without him knowing about it."

"I'm positive he didn't shoplift," Blister said.

Frank turned off the main street onto Chestnut Street, heading toward Acorn.

"We'll go to the new house now and you can help me unpack this load, and then you're free to do whatever you need to do about Jonah."

He pulled the car up to a frame house at the corner of Acorn and Chestnut and turned off the engine.

Blister had only seen the house once, at night, and she

was surprised to see how bright and happy it was, painted the soft orange color of cantaloupe. It had a wide porch, a huge maple tree in the front yard, and a long backyard with a fishpond.

"Home sweet home!" Frank said, hopping out of the truck.

The one time Blister had been inside the house was right after the former owners had moved out and the place was cold and smelling of raccoons. She had glanced at the living room then, with its big stone fireplace and bank of windows, and looked into the master bedroom on the second floor, with its own private bath and a small fireplace. Then she'd run up to the third floor, which was to be her bedroom, an attic room, the roof pitched, the walls full of bookcases, a tiny bathroom with a standing shower and an overhead fan.

She loved the room. It was hidden away from the rest of the house like the room she'd had in the old farmhouse when she was a little girl, before her baby sister was born dead, before Jack Reed left.

But she wasn't exactly happy to move out of the

apartment where she had lived with her mother and no one else but Daisy G. visiting on weekends.

Now Frank Holt would be in her mother's bedroom and at the dinner table and in front of the television every night and it would never be the same.

She followed Frank through the front door.

"It's a little musty because the furnace hasn't been on and it's been empty for a month or so, but look at this living room with the window seat and fireplace." He extended his arm toward the fireplace. "Pretty great, don't you think?"

She followed him down the hall to the kitchen, which was small but had glass doors all along the back of the house overlooking the fishpond.

"We're getting fish," Frank said. "We'll clean it out and put in fresh water and some plants and buy some beauties at the pet store. Gold and red and black-striped and bright yellow. You'll love it."

He turned on the faucet in the kitchen and splashed water on his face.

"And here's the dining room and then a family

room. I bet you never thought you'd have a family room, did you?"

"I never thought I wanted one."

"Well, you've got one now whether you wanted it or not."

What Blister wanted, what she had always wanted, was a family. Her own family, the one she'd had with her mother and father when she was a little girl. Even though her parents had been divorced for almost two years, the longing for them to be together didn't go away.

"Can we get the boxes out of the truck now?" She headed back outside to unload the boxes. "I'm feeling in a hurry to find Jonah just in case he's still in town."

"I wanted to show you your room," Frank said.

"I saw it when I came with Mom the first time," Blister said.

"Well?"

"It's a great room," she said.

"I'm going to get you something for it," Frank said, following her outside.

"Like what?"

"Like maybe your own telephone."

She started to say she'd rather have a cell phone but stopped herself. Frank Holt was trying too hard, but trying to make her happy nevertheless.

When they came inside with the first load of boxes for the living room, the phone in the kitchen was ringing and Frank answered.

Blister stopped to listen.

"The Cranes have moved," Frank was saying. "We're Frank Holt and Mary Reed and Blister. The phone company is putting in our new number today."

She smiled in spite of herself. It was the first time Frank had called her Blister.

"Well, that's nice," he was saying. "Come on over anytime you want after tomorrow when we'll be moved in. Today is moving day."

"Who was that?"

"Someone your age who lives across the street. I didn't get his name."

They unpacked the rest of the truck, stacking the books and CDs and couch pillows and small chairs in the living room. There was a ficus tree and the rocker, which Jack Reed had given Mary, and Blister's baby chair with a needlepoint seat of Jack and Jill. There were boxes of photographs in black frames, which her mother would hang on the wall, and knickknacks and a picture Daisy G. had painted of the farmhouse where they used to live.

"The movers will pick up the big stuff," Frank was saying. "I think I've only got about two more loads."

Blister watched Frank bring in a load of boxes, three heavy ones at once, half covering his face.

He was a big man with thick, firm arms and large hands. Sometimes she could see why her mother liked him. He could take care of things. Chop wood and build a bed and fix the plumbing. Mary Reed was nervous about things and had trouble feeling safe and Frank would help her. Blister knew that.

Outside, standing on the front porch while Frank brought in another load of boxes, she checked the neighborhood. It was a pretty street with cleaned-up yards and bicycles leaning against the porch railings and fresh paint on the shutters. Two boys were riding their bikes down the middle of the street with their legs straight out in either direction, riding no hands, no helmets, baseball caps on backwards.

A woman, probably a mother, was shouting at them from down the street in the yard of a yellow-brick house.

"Harry," she was calling. "Put your hands on the handlebars or I'll confiscate the bike."

Harry rode on with his friend past Blister as she climbed into the back of the pickup truck. Two small boxes were left, one sealed with masking tape, the other tied with rope, a stuffed white rabbit with hardly any fur coming out of the space between the flaps. Millie was the rabbit's name, and every time Blister tried to toss the rabbit, Mary Reed would retrieve her from the trash.

"She's your childhood," her mother would say to her. "Millie's been with you through thick and thin."

Blister stuffed Millie back in the box, picked up the two boxes, and climbed out of the truck. She walked up the stairs to the porch and sat down on the railing to take a break.

Across the street, a boy was lying on the wide railings of the front porch of a house painted green with black shutters and white trim. He was wearing jeans and a sweatshirt and had his one leg crossed over the other at the ankle. His head was on the railing and he was holding a long stick of incense, a whisper of smoke lifting in the air above his face, the sweet smell of incense traveling across the street.

He turned his head toward Blister, sat up, his legs dangling over the porch railing, and dropped the incense, still lit, over the railing.

"Are you the new family who's moving in?"

Blister nodded.

"Do you go to Memorial Junior High?"

He'd hopped off the porch and was crossing his yard, coming toward the street.

"Do I know you?" he asked, sauntering in her direction, one shoulder lower than the other.

"I know you," Blister said.

It was Jakob Cutter.

6

Searching for Jonah

jakob Cutter crossed the street and stopped just short of the lawn in front of Blister's new house, his hands in his pockets, his head cocked just so, as if he had been practicing *cool* in the mirror.

"Private property unless you invite me over, right?" he asked. He took a stick of gum out of his pocket, dropped the wrapper on the ground, and stuffed the gum in his mouth.

"I'm not inviting you," Blister said, swinging her legs over the railings, gripping the wood so she wouldn't lose her balance.

Slowly, as if she'd had a concussion and her brain was beginning to clear, she realized that Jakob Cutter lived across the street from her new house.

"Did anyone tell you someone died in your house last winter?"

She kept her head down, looking at the ground, feeling faint, almost sick.

"Just thought you'd want to know," he said, turning his baseball cap around backwards.

"Is that your dad?" he asked, indicating Frank Holt, who was visible in the window of the living room unpacking boxes.

"No, he's not my dad."

"He's the mover guy, yeah?" He folded his arms across his chest, taking Blister's arrival on Acorn Street under advisement. "So who's going to be living here?"

"Just my family. Me and my mother and the mover guy."

"That's it?"

"That's it," Blister said, wondering what she should say to him now with all that had happened, whether to bring up Jonah or pretend she didn't know what had gone on at the bus station. Or say she'd seen the story about him in the paper, as if she believed the nameless

Memorial Junior High student shoplifter was actually Jakob Cutter.

And then Jakob brought up Jonah himself.

"You're Jonah's friend, right?"

"His best friend," Blister said, to set the story straight, so Jakob Cutter would have no question about Blister's loyalties.

"Did you know he got arrested for stealing?"

"I heard that. But he didn't steal."

"He had a load of electronic stuff in his backpack." Jakob took a stick of incense from his back pocket and stuck it behind his ear. "I don't know how it could have gotten in the backpack without his help."

He stepped up on the lawn, leaning against a lamp-post in the front yard.

"Have you seen him since?"

"I see him all the time. Almost every day."

"Today?" he asked.

She didn't answer. Blister wasn't going to tell Jakob Cutter anything, not about Jonah disappearing or the missing-child report that Ms. Morrison had filed or how desperate Jonah was to belong to Jakob's group of popular friends. She had to be careful to protect herself and Jonah. Jakob Cutter was smart and cunning and could cause trouble for her too.

"So when you see Jonah, tell him I feel for him," Jakob said. "I'll see you later."

But he didn't leave. He stood on the front lawn watching Blister head into the house. She could feel his eyes on her back.

"Hey, Blister," he called.

She turned around.

"Weird you moving in across the street. It could've been anyone, right?"

Frank had unpacked the book boxes and filled the built-in bookshelves around the fireplace. He was just stacking the empty boxes when Blister walked back in the house.

"Who died in this house last winter?" she asked, coming into the living room.

"Who told you someone died?" Frank asked.

"The creep who lives across the street."

She pointed to Jakob, who was walking up the steps to his porch and through the front door to his house.

"You know him?"

"Not exactly *know* him, but I know about him."

She helped Frank break down the boxes and stack them.

"He's one of the guys that Jonah follows around hoping to be part of their crowd," Blister said. "I'm sure he was at the bus station when Jonah got accused of stealing."

She opened one of the boxes of CDs.

"So who died?"

"A family called Crane lived here with two teenage boys and a single mother and a grandmother. The grandmother died."

Blister leaned against the door.

"Of what?"

"She was old. That's what I heard. Very old and ill."

"Do you know which room she died in?"

"Not in the attic room," Frank said. "You're perfectly

safe from her ghost sleeping upstairs. Probably the room where she died is the one next to our bedroom."

Our bedroom, Blister thought. The picture of her mother and Frank Holt in a room called *our bedroom* made her suddenly angry.

"My *mother's* bedroom."

"That is also true," Frank said gently, not willing to rise to a fight.

"Can we go now?" she asked.

"We can," Frank said.

Meeting Jakob had made her anxious about Jonah, about searching for him before it was too late and he had disappeared for good.

Jonah was capable of that, she thought. His imagination was so enormous that he sometimes couldn't separate the truth from what he imagined to be true. She never knew exactly what he might do next.

"Get your stuff, and I've got one more trip back to the apartment to pick up your mom and the rest of the boxes."

Blister followed him out of the house, hopped up in

the truck, and rested her feet — in bright green sneakers — on the dashboard.

Through the window of Jakob's house she saw a woman who must have been Jakob's mother standing in the living room with a baby over her shoulder. That surprised her. Jakob didn't seem at all the sort of boy to live in the same house with a baby.

"So I'm dropping you off at the Morrisons'?" Frank asked.

"Drop me at Bixley Elementary instead."

"Who's there?"

"Maybe no one since it's a Saturday."

"But you're hoping for Jonah?"

"I just have a hunch," Blister said.

Jonah hated change. After Thomas Hale left the family and moved to Boston without warning and the Morrisons moved to North Haven, Connecticut, all Jonah wanted was to put his life back together the way it used to be. Even when he decided to do his own television show, what he hoped for, more than becoming famous, was that Thomas Hale would see the show and he'd be so impressed by Jonah that he'd come back to the family.

Maybe Jonah had even missed her, Blister thought. Maybe he missed the hours they used to spend together last year in sixth grade, meeting at her house and his house, in homeroom, and behind the science projects after school when all the rest of the students had left except the janitor and the kids who were in detention.

"Jonah and I spent a lot of time together last year when we were innocent."

"Innocent!" Frank laughed. "You're still innocent."

"I haven't been anything like innocent since I started junior high."

"But that was only a month ago."

"Things change very fast in junior high."

Blister had been thinking about change. Just in the last month since junior high started and Frank Holt decided to be part of the family, she'd been on a whirli-gig, holding on as tight as she could, feeling she could fly apart, afraid of losing control. And she had always been a strong and steady girl. Even when bad things happened to her, she could count on herself.

Frank pulled up to the curb in front of Bixley Elementary.

"Looks pretty empty. Do you want me to wait to see if the doors are unlocked?"

"It's okay," Blister said. "I know the back way in."

"So when will we see you?" Frank asked as Blister opened the truck door.

"I'm going to look around the school and if no one's there or I decide not to go to the Morrisons', then I'll call you."

"Just stay in touch."

Frank handed her some change — four quarters, some dimes, and three dollar bills.

"Bus fare, telephone change, and a candy bar," he said.

Blister took the bills and stuffed them in the pocket of her shorts, a surprising softness in her feelings for Frank taking hold of her. Her father hadn't paid attention in the last few years since he met Tamara. He had a habit of forgetting his wallet if they went out to dinner and when the bill came, he would reach into his back pocket, shake his head, and look up at Blister with a boyish expression of bewilderment.

"Did you happen to bring some dough, Alyssa, sweet-heart?" he'd ask. "I seem to have left my wallet at home on the dresser."

Blister carried her own wallet when she went out to dinner with her father.

"See you," Blister called, jumping out of the truck.

"Thanks for coming with me and the boxes," Frank said. "It's a good beginning to our new lives."

It was sunny and warm for October but the air felt unsteady, as if at any moment the weather could change. Even in the sun, she felt a chill and wrapped her arms around her chest for warmth.

One thing she knew about Jonah Morrison was that wherever he had hidden himself, he was imagining a plan. The plan might be impossible — probably it was impossible — but he would try to make it happen.

Sitting on the front steps of Bixley Elementary, her bottom cold from the cement, she closed her eyes and thought about Jonah hidden someplace, maybe cold.

Certainly he would be very hungry and scared. For a kind of fat, dreamy boy who wore his pants too high and his sneakers from Wal-Mart, Jonah Morrison was brave. A brave nerd is how Blister thought of him. He could think up a big story, something outrageous, a plan like *JONAH, THE WHALE*, the kids' talk show for television.

If Jonah dreamed a story, he could walk right into the middle and make it his own.

Somewhere in North Haven, Connecticut, or maybe another town, even New York City, Jonah was scheming.

If he left North Haven, he'd go by train and not the bus. He'd never go back to the bus station next to Ram's Electronics.

He might call Thomas Hale in Boston to brag that one of his friends had stolen some electronic equipment and he, Jonah Morrison the Brave, was willing to take the blame. He would never say that he'd been tricked by the boys he longed to have as his friends. He'd tell Thomas Hale that he chose to take the blame because he was strong and generous.

Once Jonah got to where he was going, New York or

Boston or even Montana, Blister guessed he'd change his name. He'd call himself an orphan and make up dead parents and a baby sister who had died at birth, like Blister's baby sister, Lila Rose.

He'd say he went to school in Canada and had come to Connecticut for his aunt's funeral in North Haven.

He'd say he had had a successful television show and was now planning to move to Los Angeles to work in the movies.

Jonah didn't think of himself as a liar. He thought of his stories as true because they were about him and he'd been the one to make them up.

And just as she was having fantasies about Jonah's whereabouts, she suddenly knew that he wouldn't leave North Haven. Instinct told her that. Instinct was Blister's secret weapon.

Somewhere unexpected, Jonah was hiding. Because he had a very busy imagined life with enough friends traveling through his mind to keep him interested, he could hide for a long time without coming out.

Blister walked up the last set of stairs to the school. She expected the building to be locked on a Saturday, but the door was open and she went in. At the end of the main corridor, the janitor, Mr. Young, looked up from mopping the floor.

"I recognize you by your red hair and it's still red," he said, shaking his head. "Some red hair."

Laughter was coming from the kindergarten room where the children in costume were practicing for a Halloween play. Blister watched them through the window on the door.

"You better hurry along and get done whatever you're here to do," Mr. Young said. "Those children are leaving soon and then I'm locking up and you don't want to spend the night in this school."

"I'm just checking my last year's homeroom to see if I left something," Blister said, heading toward the stairs to the second floor where the upper grades were located.

"Hope you didn't leave your brain," Mr. Young said, laughing hard, very pleased with himself. "You're going to need it."

Upstairs were the fifth and sixth grades, the assembly room, and the art and music rooms. Blister walked all the way to the end of the corridor where the sixth-grade classroom was, opened the glass door, and went in.

There was something clean and cozy about an empty school, Blister was thinking. Like reading her first chapter books without pictures when she was little and realizing that a story without pictures belonged only to her. She felt as if she owned the whole floor where she had spent the last year, trying to be a cheerleader and failing, trying to be popular and failing, wishing her family back together, wishing to be famous.

She felt older this morning than she had been only last year, less than four months ago when she graduated sixth grade. It was as if the desks had shrunk in her absence, the blackboards lowered for kids smaller than herself, and the compositions displayed on the bulletin board, which she stopped to read, seemed to be written by children.

She picked up a piece of chalk and wrote JONAH MORRISON on the blackboard. Then in capital letters she added RETSILB, which was how she signed her name when she first took on the name Blister, writing from right to left and backwards.

The books were neatly stacked, the desks in straight, formal lines. The back wall, reserved for social studies projects, was plastered with photographs of Central America. Her desk had been in the third row from the window, fourth row back, and she sat down at it, put her feet in the green sneakers on the desk chair in front of her, and reached into the desk. She found a penny with something gummy like jam all over it, a notebook with drawings of animals with the heads of girls, a math book, and a piece of dried fudge. She sniffed the old fudge and put it back where she found it, reminded that she was starving.

It was strange to go back, like walking backwards without turning your head so you can't see where you're going. She was dizzy, as if the oxygen had gone out of the sixth-grade classroom in her absence. Strange to sit in the chair where she had sat, in the same room where she had been, but no longer be the same person. Not very different, but older, with troubling things to think about, like Frank Holt and Jonah and Jakob Cutter.

There was no sign of Alyssa Reed, alias Blister, on this desk where she had worked and daydreamed for a year, passing notes back and forth with Jonah Morrison. So much time to spend in one place without leaving a single footprint. She should have written BLISTER with red indelible marker on the inside of the desk so other kids would know that she had been there.

Jonah had sat one desk up and two across so Blister could sit in math class and look at the back of his head as it bobbed back and forth, sometimes falling to the desk fast asleep. They passed their notes from Jonah to Billy Frame to Sara Gander to Blister and back again.

Big plans today. Meet me after school. J. Morrison, Esq.

Amazing surprise coming after lunch. You won't believe it so meet me on the playground. J. Morrison, Esq.

I just found out some fantastic news. You'll be EXCITED to death. Meet me at the drugstore. J. Morrison, Esq.

Great, Blister would write back. *I'll be there after school.* Or *I'll meet you on the playground.*

Or *I'll see you at the drugstore with your fantastic news. Love, Blister*

She felt out of place returning to Bixley, not altogether comfortable. And lonely because elementary school was over and it would never be the same again no matter how many times she came back to visit.

The last time she'd seen Jonah was a week ago Monday before the bell for assembly. He was leaning against his locker, his hands in his pockets, and when he saw Blister, he turned away.

"I'm not poison," she had said as she walked past him on her way to homeroom. "Just in case you were worried."

But she had a sinking feeling in her stomach that she had lost him completely and turned back to see if he was looking at her. Which he was not.

Still, she was wise to return to Bixley to look for Jonah Morrison. It would be typical of him to go back to the place where he had almost been happy, almost famous, almost popular, and well-known for his wild imagination.

If she was right, Jonah Morrison was somewhere in the building, hiding out, hoping she was looking for him.

When Ms. Bralove, the old art teacher, who was now the new sixth-grade teacher, rushed into the classroom wearing tight jeans, high-top tennis shoes, and a baseball cap, Blister was putting the old piece of fudge in the pocket of her jeans.

"So what are you doing at school on a Saturday?" Ms. Bralove asked. "I'd have thought you had better things to do."

Blister wasn't prepared with an answer.

"Are you meeting someone?" Ms. Bralove asked, searching through her desk drawer. "I never come here on weekends but I left my cell phone."

"I'm just sitting here thinking."

"They're going to lock up soon," Ms. Bralove said. "Don't want to spend the weekend locked in and hungry."

"The kindergarten is practicing for a play."

"So I saw."

"They won't lock up until the kindergarten is finished, isn't that right?"

"Sounds right." Ms. Bralove found her cell phone in one of the desk drawers. "So keep track of time." She walked to the door with her tiny mincing steps, her head shaking back and forth as if she were listening to rock music, already dialing on her cell.

"Ms. Bralove?"

She nodded without looking up from her phone.

"You haven't seen Jonah Morrison around, have you?"

"Do I know Jonah Morrison?"

"You know him because he had that TV program called *JONAH, THE WHALE*," Blister said.

"Jeez." Ms. Bralove threw up her hands. "Who didn't know *JONAH, THE WHALE*?"

"I was his sidekick," Blister said, wishing to be a part of the success story. "Sort of like his assistant."

"I remember. I used to think, *There's a cute-looking boy if he'd lose some weight.* No, I haven't seen him all year so I assume he's gone to junior high and forgotten all about us."

And she waved, heading out the door and talking on her cell phone to someone called Neddy.

After Ms. Bralove left, Blister walked around the room, not much of a room unless the kids were there — a few bulletin boards, some papier-mâché Latina dancers hanging from the ceiling, an American flag folded on top of the bookcase, a science project with amphibians, nothing of particular interest since the subjects were the same ones Blister had studied last year.

When she saw Jonah, she'd tell him that Bixley was hollow and strange without him.

If she ever saw Jonah again.

And if she did see him, she planned to say that she had always been a loyal friend to him and he wasn't worth the time of day, as Daisy G. would say.

She checked the window overlooking the front of the school. No one was milling around the steps except the janitor smoking a cigarette. The kindergartners must still be rehearsing for their show.

The clock above Ms. Bralove's desk said one-thirty. No wonder her stomach was growling. By now, the movers had taken the furniture to the new house on Acorn Street. Her mother would be riding on the bench seat of Frank's truck, pushed way over so her shoulders rubbed up next to his, her hand on his upper thigh. That's how they drove around, with Blister squished in the tiny

84

backseat, wishing she could throw up on demand so they'd understand how they made her feel, kissing in the front seat when the truck stopped at a red light.

One more walk around the room, she told herself, and then she'd head to the Morrisons' apartment to see if Jonah had possibly changed his mind and called home.

At the back of the room, next to a bank of windows overlooking the woods behind the school, was a supply closet usually kept locked so the kids wouldn't help themselves to the cartons of apple juice and boxes of graham crackers for snacks. But when Blister turned the knob, the door opened and light from the windows flooded the closet. Stacks of paper and pencils and paperclips and cups lined the walls; literature and science and math books shared the shelves with paper towels and graham crackers and apple juice and packages of pretzels. But the back of the closet was too dark to see, even with daylight spilling in from the windows. The shelves were so piled with cleaning materials and mops and brooms and canisters of lemonade mix that she couldn't make out anything beyond supplies.

She got down on her hands and knees to look around,

checking the cleaning supplies and the boxes holding books for the spring semester.

At the very back of the closet, she came upon two tennis shoes attached to legs in corduroy pants.

Blister reached out to touch the corduroy pants.

"Jonah?"

"Hi," he whispered.

She sat back on her haunches, staring into the darkness, unable to make out his face.

"It's me," he said. "Can't you tell?"

"Jonah, you dope!" she said. "What in the world are you doing in corduroy pants like some kind of nerd when all you want in your whole life is to be popular?"

7

Time Out in the Closet

S o I guess you know what's happened?" Jonah said, wiggling over so Blister would have room to sit down.

"It was in the newspaper this morning."

"With my name?"

"I just knew it was you."

"They aren't allowed to use my name in the newspaper. It's against the law."

"They can't use your name because you're underage, even though they probably wanted to."

"I didn't shoplift."

"I know."

"You don't know everything, Blister," he said. "I could have shoplifted if I wanted to."

"I don't think so," she said. "You'd be too chicken."

She inched away, just far enough that she could catch a glimpse of Jonah's soft, fleshy profile in the corner of her eye. She was still angry at him and her feelings were still hurt, but mainly what she felt was relief, so happy to have found him and pleased with herself for knowing where he might be that she couldn't separate one feeling from the other.

"Are you going to tell me what happened?"

Blister pulled a stack of art paper under her so the floor didn't feel so hard, and they closed the door in case the janitor came to check on Blister, opened a box of graham crackers, pushed aside the cleaning supplies, and settled back against the wall of the closet. Jonah started to talk.

"I'll tell you everything if you don't interrupt me."

"I never interrupt you."

"Sometimes you make fun of me."

"Just tell me the story," Blister said.

Jonah Morrison tended to speak as if his life story came from a book he had read in which the hero, Jonah, has terrible things happen to him, comes upon great dangers, has many near-death experiences, and in the end, triumphs over evil and adversity to become famous once again.

Which is how he told his story of shoplifting, his shoulders damp with perspiration, pressed against Blister's.

"So Jonah Morrison left school on Friday afternoon the second week in October with plans to spend the evening downtown with his best friends, Jakob Cutter and Eddie James and Monster Bar. You probably know," he added, "that they're the most popular guys at Memorial Junior High."

"This time tell the whole and complete truth," Blister said.

"This is the truth. What you are about to hear is the whole and complete truth, so help me God."

"Then don't call yourself Jonah Morrison. Call yourself I."

"I *am* Jonah Morrison."

Blister put her hands over her ears. Sometimes he drove her so crazy she thought her brain might fly out of the top of her head.

They were sitting in the dark with the door closed and it didn't exactly smell as if Jonah had changed his clothes in the last couple of days, so Blister draped her arm over her nose to muffle the smell of too much popcorn and bad breath.

"Go on," she said.

"So these guys were headed to the bus station to hang out."

"And you went along with them."

"Right. They said they were going to hang out and maybe see a movie and why didn't I come along."

"So they invited you, right?"

Jonah hesitated.

"Did you follow them or did they invite you?" Blister asked.

She didn't mind Jonah's amazing stories — they were one of the things she loved about him. But sometimes, like this time, it was important to tell the exact truth, which was hard for Jonah to do.

"Sort of both," Jonah began and then his voice dropped, "but I mostly followed them."

"To the bus station."

"They had chocolate candies with white cream and cherries inside and they gave me one, but I didn't eat it, thinking if I did and it made me throw up, then they'd probably laugh."

"Why would it make you throw up?"

"Because of the poison. Someone could've decided to put poison in the chocolate."

"Someone like these guys who were your friends?"

"As a practical joke. They wouldn't really want to hurt me," he said.

The closet was hot and streams of salty water ran down their faces.

"So we were hanging around the bus station, me with my empty backpack except for twenty dollars I'd saved, and they were balancing chocolate candy on the ends of their tongues and joking that they were planning to rob the electronics store."

"Did they ask *you* to rob the electronics store for them?"

Jonah pushed farther down against the wall so he was practically lying down.

"Sort of."

"And you said NO?"

"Sort of."

"What is 'sort of no'?"

"I said, 'Listen guys, maybe I will and maybe I won't but not now, maybe not even today.'"

"That was stupid."

"Right."

"Then what?"

"We were just hanging out and they were talking about the things they did on the weekends, like drive without a license and steal candy from Harly's Drugs and make out with girls behind the shed on the playground, that sort of stuff."

"And you said you did that stuff too?"

"I said I did some stuff."

"Like what?"

"Like, you know."

"I don't know. Like make out with girls?"

"That kind of thing."

"Do you make out with girls or don't you?" Blister asked, beginning to wonder if shy, awkward Jonah Morrison had actually changed that much.

"I'm getting mixed up," Jonah said. "You're talking too fast and jumbling up my brain."

"Do you steal candy or drive cars without a license or make out at recess in the athletic shed?"

"I think about making out," Jonah said quietly.

"But you told them you DID IT. Not that you thought about it."

"Sort of."

"So who robbed the electronics store?"

Jonah took a deep breath and when he finally spoke it was in a whisper, as if someone were pressed against the supply room door listening to their conversation.

"I was just standing there, leaning against the wall of the bus station, wondering if I looked more or less cool, like less cool than Jakob but maybe more cool than Monster Bar, and then they must have left and I didn't even notice they were gone since I was thinking about how I looked when all of a sudden a bunch of things happened." His breath shook in his throat like wind in a tunnel.

"So Jakob leaned up real close to me and said something I couldn't understand and then he ran and so did Monster Bar and the next thing I knew two policemen were towering over me with their sticks and guns."

"With their guns? Is that true?"

"With their sticks and they picked up my backpack, which had been sitting right beside me on the sidewalk with nothing in it but my wallet, and they lifted it up to examine it and there was all this electronic equipment in MY backpack so I almost died of a heart attack."

"Of course you did," Blister said.

"And then they asked me some questions and I said I had NOT stolen the electronics and they asked why it was in my backpack and I said I hadn't a clue and they didn't believe me."

"Very surprising," Blister said quietly.

"That's what I thought," Jonah said. "Very surprising they should think that I, Jonah Morrison, had stolen the electronic equipment since I had already earned plenty of money with my TV show."

"Our TV show," Blister said.

"My idea."

"Never mind. You didn't earn any money with the TV show."

"There's no way the police would know that."

"Why do you think the police knew who you were?"

"I was on television, Blister."

Blister put her hands over her ears again, and shook her head back and forth to shake out everything that Jonah was saying in his own defense.

"Did anything else happen?" Blister asked.

"Of course," Jonah went on, his voice assuming a kind of calm confidence. "I was unjustly accused of shoplifting. The police took down my name and telephone number and school, and then they called my mother, who was brokenhearted, and they made her pick me up at the police station."

"And what happened after that?"

"My mother came with Quentin, who was sleeping on her shoulder, and she didn't talk to me on the bus coming home, and then she made me cocoa and I went to bed and didn't sleep."

"So when did you run away from home?"

"After breakfast while Mama was at the market with Quentin buying apple juice and diapers. I couldn't *prove* to the police that I hadn't stolen the electronics, so I *had* to run away."

He leaned up so close that Blister could feel the heat of his breath.

"So here I am where you have found me," he said. "How did you know I'd be here?"

"I guessed you'd only go as far as your last happiness, and that was last year in the sixth-grade class at Bixley, when you were famous and we were best friends."

For a long time, Blister and Jonah sat on the floor silent, thinking of nothing in particular, Jonah leaning into her so she felt the weight of his body even though they were sitting side by side.

It must be almost three o'clock, Blister thought. Daisy G. would be at her modern dance class and her mother was probably in the living room of their new house, telling the movers where to put the furniture and unpacking books. Maybe Jakob Cutter was sitting on the railing of his front porch watching Mary Reed. By nighttime, the Reed family should be completely moved into the new house, and Daisy G. would have driven back to her house in the country and Blister's father, Jack Reed, would be calling to make arrangements for her to spend the night in his new apartment with him and Tamara and her white French poodle, Ann-Renee.

"We need to make a plan," Blister said.

"I don't want to make a plan." Jonah finished the box of graham crackers. "I'm staying here for maybe the rest of my life."

Blister drew her knees up under her chin and rested her head on them.

"How will you eat?"

"You'll get food and bring it here."

"Every day?"

"Of course. I have to eat every day."

"And you'll stay in the supply closet during the week when the kids are around?"

"I'll have to move around during the day. Maybe I'll go to the basement or the little room behind the gym where the music stuff is kept. I've checked out the whole school. There are plenty of places to hide, even a very good place under the stage in the auditorium where nobody would ever think to look."

"I don't think it'll work, Jonah. I think you have to go home and just tell the truth about what happened."

"I told the truth and the police didn't believe me because, as they said, I had a backpack full of electronic

97

equipment and how could I explain that? They don't know me. They think I'm just like every other kid who hangs out at the bus station."

"You're not like any other kid, Jonah, so tell that to the police," Blister said softly. "You're just yourself."

8

Foraging for Jonah

blister slipped out the front door of Bixley Elementary just as the kindergartners were leaving with their parents, whose cars were parked along the curb. She hurried down the steps, walked quickly along the sidewalk where the cars, their engines running, were parked, and would have missed Frank Holt's Chevrolet pickup truck if Frank hadn't shouted, "BLISTER!" at the top of his voice so that the kindergartners stopped in their tracks and looked.

"Where the hell have you been?"

He pulled out of his parking place.

"We've been worried sick. Your mother and I kept driving by the school and your mother came in and asked the janitor if you were here and he said he'd seen you but you were long gone."

"I was here, exactly where you dropped me off."

"It's almost four o'clock. We called Ms. Morrison."

"That's where I'm going now. To Ms. Morrison's."

"No, you're not going to Ms. Morrison's. You're coming to the new house with me and helping us unpack and then you'll be spending the night at your father's and Tamara's apartment."

Blister pressed her nose against the closed window of the truck. She had plans. Unpacking the boxes at the new house was not included among them.

Her first plan was to go to Aker's Market across the street from Jonah's apartment, buy enough food to last a day or two, and take it back to Jonah by five o'clock, when he would be waiting for her by the back door of the school. Mr. Young, the janitor, would have left and locked the doors.

"Frank," she began in her most reasonable voice. "I have to go to Ms. Morrison's to tell her what I know."

"What do you know?"

"Nothing."

"You didn't find Jonah."

"No, I didn't."

Blister was not a good liar, but this was an emergency and in an emergency, she could lie.

"Well, I'm sorry about that. I was hoping you were on the right track," Frank said. "Maybe the police will find him."

"Maybe you'll let me go to Ms. Morrison's and tell her personally that I looked and didn't find him."

"You could call her on the phone."

There was a long silence and Blister didn't reply, but she noticed that Frank had turned left on Anderson Avenue, away from Acorn Street and in the direction of the Morrisons' apartment complex.

"I'll drop you off, drive over to check the old apartment to be sure the movers didn't leave anything, and pick you up in fifteen minutes," Frank said.

Which was just enough time for Blister to stop by the Morrisons'. She knocked on the door, but as she expected, no one answered. Then she ran down the street to Aker's Market to buy raisins and milk and nuts and bananas and apples and yogurt, stuffed them into her backpack, and was waiting in front of the Morrisons' apartment when Frank Holt drove up.

"Did you see Ms. Morrison?" Frank asked.

"No one answered the door."

"So you'll call her later and we'll head home now."

"Can we first stop by Bixley Elementary? I left my English book on my old desk, so if you could just drop me by, it'll only take a minute," Blister said.

"Can't that wait until tomorrow?"

"Tomorrow's Sunday and it'll be closed. I promise, I'll only be gone a minute."

Blister ran around the school, up the back steps of Bixley, and knocked on the door. Jonah must have had his ear against it because the door flew open and there he was, his mouth and corduroy trousers covered with graham cracker crumbs, his cheeks red from the heat inside the supply closet.

"Dinner!" Blister said, opening her backpack, handing him the stash of groceries. "So I'll be back tomorrow in the afternoon at exactly two o'clock when my mom and Frank are at the movies."

"And I'll be exactly here at this door unless there's some emergency."

"I'll bring some M&M's. Maybe something better."

Blister leaned over to hug him, throwing her arms around his neck. But instead of burrowing his head next to hers, he kept his face forward so their faces met, accidentally, awkwardly, and he kissed her, heading for her lips but missing, kissing her on her chin.

"'Bye." Blister backed away. "See you."

"I love you, Blister," Jonah said, the weight of his emotion thick in the autumn air.

Later Blister thought she should have said, "I love you too" or "I like you too," either one. But neither was exactly true, something in-between. She turned around, without looking back at Jonah, and ran down the steps along the side of the building to Frank Holt's truck, her heart beating in her mouth.

In the truck, she reached up and touched her face

where Jonah had kissed her, leaving graham cracker crumbs on her chin, a funny feeling like hunger in her stomach.

Of course she was hungry. All she'd had to eat all day was graham crackers.

"Are you okay?" Frank asked.

"I'm fine," Blister said.

Maybe she was hungry, Blister thought, or maybe the feeling in her stomach was a different kind of empty. She wished that Jonah hadn't kissed her. She wasn't expecting that. She wasn't ready.

"Your father called. He'll be picking you up at about six," Frank said. "Taking you to the movies and then out to dinner."

"With Tamara?"

"He didn't say."

"I have to sleep on a couch in their living room when I spend the night because the bedroom is getting redecorated. Fixed up for me, my dad says, but it's really for Tamara's mom when she comes to visit with the fur coats and silver dazzle dresses she likes to wear to church."

Frank reached over and patted Blister's arm — a light touch and his hand was back on the steering wheel — but just the sympathetic gesture made her eyes fill with tears.

She leaned back against the headrest and squeezed her eyes shut.

"Okay?" Frank asked.

"Fine," she replied.

"Too many people crowding you out of your own life," he said.

Frank was right. She had Jonah and Jakob Cutter and her father and Tamara and her mother and Frank pressing her in ways she couldn't explain in words because there were no words. She was losing a vision of what she wanted for herself.

Jakob Cutter was sitting on his front steps when the truck pulled up in front of the new house on Acorn Street.

"So that's the boy you told me about this morning," Frank said.

"The creep of all creeps."

"He came over to ask where you were."

"If he comes again, tell him he isn't welcome."

She hopped down from the truck and walked across the front yard, feeling Jakob Cutter's eyes on her back. When she got in the house where her mother was organizing books on the back of the sofa, she checked the window in the living room and there he was, headed across the street toward her house.

"See that boy on his way over here?" she asked Mary Reed.

"I've already met him."

"Could you please tell him I'm busy?"

"He's only interested in being friendly to a new neighbor, Alyssa. He was very polite to me when he came over."

"He faked it. He fakes everything."

Blister had a clear eye for what was genuine and what was not. Jonah Morrison was genuine even though he told lies. Jakob was the real liar, pretending to be someone he wasn't, like a good, kind, thoughtful, decent, sweet seventh-grade boy.

Blister ran upstairs to her room, shut the door, and locked it.

The room was large and full of light. Even at dusk, the gray light striped the floor pale yellow. Her bed was under a skylight above the trees and when she lay on her back all she could see was a gray-blue canvas of sky.

It was quiet and peaceful and although Blister didn't ordinarily like peaceful — too slow and dull and lonely for an only child — this afternoon, after Jonah Morrison had just missed kissing her on the lips, she was glad to be alone.

She needed to think so her muddy mind, usually as clear as spring water, could settle.

Downstairs she could hear the sound of voices and imagined Jakob Cutter was in the kitchen, winning her mother's affection.

In a box next to the bed were her blue cloud sheets and pillowcases and the white comforter from her old room. Blister opened it, but she wasn't ready to make her bed yet. Only to lie on it, which she did, watching the sky grow grayer as the sun fell, and the coming of dark.

What Blister knew of romance was everything she'd heard and read. A lot, but not enough to understand exactly what happened between a girl and boy. She could imagine what went on, like in the movies. But she couldn't exactly understand what actually happened, so her thinking about romance was more like a picture on the screen of her mind than an actual experience.

After all, she couldn't tell someone what it was like to eat a piece of lemon meringue pie — her very favorite food, Daisy G.'s specialty — if the person had never tasted lemon meringue. She could say it's yummy and sweet and a little tart and thick with lemon in your mouth and airy with meringue. But saying all of that would not be lemon meringue.

Blister had books, mainly magazines like *True Romance* and *Teen Love*, collected in her box of Things to Keep, and she intended to read the stories sometime when she wasn't so busy with other things. She had actually read a couple since all the girls in junior high discussed romance stories and TV shows and movies as if they were personal and real.

Someday, Blister thought, she would have a boyfriend and she'd lie down on the backseat of a car with him.

But not now. She wasn't ready now.

Nevertheless, something had happened when Jonah kissed her that changed their friendship. It had only been the slightest kiss, a missed kiss, but the pure silence of the friendship that had been theirs, the safe quiet she felt when there was no conversation, was gone.

Unless she could pretend nothing had happened. Put out of mind this afternoon, go to the grocery store, buy Jonah's lunch and dinner on Sunday, slip into the back of the supply closet, and keep a distance from him. Sitting side by side, their shoulders touching all the way down their arms to their hands. Even in the dark, she should be able to draw an invisible line between their bodies.

Maybe she fell asleep. Her body grew heavy as if it were filling with air, her head foggy, her mouth dry, and the next thing she knew her mother was knocking on her bedroom door.

"Your father is here," she was saying.

She rolled out of bed, walked across the room, and lifted the lock.

"I fell asleep."

"You shouldn't lock the door. Something could happen."

"Like what?"

"Something. Anything," her mother went on as she had a habit of doing. "The house could be on fire and there you'd be, locked in your room and I couldn't get to you. Or a burglar. Just anything, Alyssa. Think about it."

"I can't think about it."

The room was dark and Blister turned on the overhead light.

"Your father is ready to take you to the movies."

"Is Tamara with him?"

"Maybe she's in the car."

"I'm not in the mood for Tamara."

"How could anyone be in the mood for Tamara?" Mary Reed said.

Blister opened her suitcase and pulled out a pair of brick-colored jeans she'd gotten on sale. She pulled a black turtleneck out of the suitcase and changed while her mother stood in the doorway, her arms folded across her chest.

"You need to tell your father that you'd like to see him sometimes without Tamara, Alyssa."

"I'll be glad to tell him."

Two years ago on the fifth of June, when Lila Rose came and went without a sound, everything changed in Blister's life. Her father moved into an apartment with Tamara. Mary Reed had what Daisy G. called a "nervous breakdown" and went to the hospital for a while.

And in protest of the changes in her life through no fault of her own, Blister stole some of Tamara's tiny clothes, lacy see-through things and strappy high heels, which she had discovered in a suitcase under her father's bed when he was still trying to keep Tamara's existence a secret.

And then on a Saturday in June just after Blister's graduation from elementary school, Jack Reed and

Tamara Gaylen got married in a boxwood garden with Ann-Renee on a tiny pink leash, washed and fluffed and perfumed, accompanying the bride down the aisle.

Jack Reed was standing in the living room talking to Frank. They didn't like each other.

"Your mother has odd taste," Jack had told Blister after he met Frank Holt for the first time. "That guy's a bull in a china shop. She likes that."

"She used to like you," Blister said.

"We were very young."

Frank never said anything about Jack Reed, good or bad. He didn't need to.

Blister ran down the first flight of stairs to the second floor and in a burst of high spirits, glad for her father to see her in her new house with a family room in an upscale neighborhood, slid down the banister to the first floor.

"Hello, Jack Reed," she said to her father. "Welcome to our mansion!"

"Nice digs, sweetie."

He kissed her on the cheek.

Her father had always called her "sweetie." She used to like it, liked the softness of the sound, the way it seemed to be a word chosen especially for her. But lately, since Tamara became the second Mrs. Jack Reed, *sweetie* had the milky, sugary sound of Hershey's chocolate.

"Ready to go?" he asked.

"Almost," Blister said.

"Almost" was what she always said when her father asked if she was ready to go. Every weekend she felt the same hesitation, as if she needed time to prepare for a change of affection.

Her father would arrive on Friday or Saturday or Sunday, depending on his schedule, to take her to his place for an overnight. He'd stand next to the front door, always awkward, making jokes. Mary Reed would ask him how he was doing and what was going on at the bowling alley, which he owned, her voice sounding whiny, as if at any moment her eyes would flood with tears. Sometimes if Frank Holt was there when Jack Reed arrived, Frank would begin to move things around — pick up the television and move it across the room, turn the couch so it was at an angle to the wall, unplug a lamp and plug it in

113

someplace else. "Taking charge" is what he called it when Mary Reed complained to him.

Blister would stand among them, a scruffy-haired pound dog was what she felt like, sensing their inexplicable disappointment in her, their dislike of one another, their unhappiness. But the best she could do was to hold her place in the room of grown-ups, refusing to yield.

"I have a plan for you tonight," Jack Reed was saying. "Tamara isn't feeling up to snuff so it'll be just you and me at the movies. And since I don't want you to catch whatever it is Tamara's coming down with, you're going to spend the night with Daisy G."

"It's fine by me," Blister said, not surprised by the change of plans, for a moment even believing her father was telling the truth and Tamara was sick. Later, alone in bed waiting for sleep, she imagined Tamara's conversation with her father. "Alyssa CAN'T spend the night," Tamara would say, stamping her little feet.

"Okay, okay," her father would have said in that way he had of backing away from trouble. "I'll tell Alyssa that you're not feeling well."

Maybe her father was always hurting her feelings. He couldn't help himself and there was nothing she could do.

Blister followed her mother upstairs.

"Tamara must have an immune-deficiency disease," Mary Reed said. "She's always sick."

"She isn't sick unless I'm coming over," Blister said, putting some clothes in her backpack, her toothbrush and toothpaste, new orangey blush, and one of Tamara's hand-me-down swing skirts. "She probably threw a temper tantrum and said she would go to her mother's if I spent the night, so Dad called Daisy G. as usual when he's in a bind and asked her to bail him out."

Blister kissed her mother good-bye.

"See you tomorrow."

They walked back downstairs together, stepping over Bewilder, who was licking her belly on the landing.

"I forgot to tell you," Mary Reed said when they got to the bottom of the stairs. "You got a present."

She followed her mother into the kitchen.

"This."

Mary Reed held up a small clear glass vase with a long-stemmed red rose.

"The boy across the street said it was a welcome-to-the-neighborhood present."

Blister had a sinking feeling in her stomach.

"Don't judge too quickly," Mary Reed said. "Maybe he isn't as bad as you think."

"Maybe he's a frog disguised as a prince," Blister said.

But it wasn't worth an argument with her mother, after all. And what did Blister really know about Jakob Cutter. Or care.

•

9

At Home in the Dance Studio

after the Reeds moved from the country to North Haven, Connecticut, after the baby and the divorce and Blister's new school, Daisy G. turned the downstairs of her old farmhouse in Clint, Connecticut, into a dance studio. She had the walls between the living room and dining room and sunporch taken down, polished the floors to a high golden honey color, hung floor-to-ceiling mirrors on three walls, and installed bars for the dancers, who came to the classes she held in her house. Usually the place was decorated for whatever Daisy G. was choreographing for her old lady dancers, who came three days a week to practice and rehearse.

When Blister arrived on Saturday night after the seven o'clock showing of *Barry Ballou and the A Team*, a

G-rated football movie at a theater crowded with ten-year-old boys, Daisy G. was choreographing *Afternoon of the Swallows*.

The studio was hung with white gauze from the ceiling, billowing with air from fans blowing around the room to give the impression of a high summer windstorm, and Daisy G. herself was in a pale blue tulle tutu and ballet slippers.

"Just in time," she said when Blister walked in. "Have you eaten dinner?"

She turned off the music and the fans.

"I made chicken à la mushrooms in white zinfandel wine sauce with a dash of butter and lemon meringue pie."

"Perfect. Of course I haven't had dinner. Dad had to go home to take care of Tamara."

Blister followed Daisy G. to the kitchen, the only room on the first floor of the farmhouse that wasn't part of the dance studio.

"I decided you need a gourmet meal."

"To make up for Tamara, who gets sick on the weekends when I'm visiting. My father's a wimp."

"Not our problem, bananafish. What's done is done and Tamara's here to stay. But we have better things to do than think about the reincarnation of Jack Reed as a wimp."

Daisy G. had set the table with candles and china plates with tiny roses around the edges and pink cloth napkins and two glasses, one for water and a wineglass for lemonade.

Everything with Daisy G. was an occasion.

"So the movie was good?"

"The movie was terrible." Blister poured herself lemonade. "I don't know why he thinks I can't see a PG movie without turning into a criminal."

Daisy G. took the chicken out of the oven, slipped a spoon into the gravy, and gave Blister a taste.

"Any luck with Jonah Morrison?" Daisy G. asked, serving a plate of chicken for Blister and herself.

"No luck yet."

She had promised Jonah not to tell anyone where he was — crossed her heart and hoped to die — which she hated to do because it might bring bad luck.

But at least she wanted to tell Daisy G. about the missed kiss.

"One of the boys with Jonah at the bus station was Jakob Cutter and it turns out he lives across the street from our new house," Blister said.

"Interesting! Have you seen him yet?"

"He brought over a vase with a rose to welcome me to the neighborhood."

"A gentleman and a prince. Very desirable."

"He's a creep and a brat."

"But you must be flattered, Alyssa," Daisy G. said. "I'm easily flattered. Roses and more roses and chocolate kisses. Those are my weaknesses."

"Jakob brought me a rose because he wants something from me. It wasn't a present for nothing in return."

"What does he want?"

"I don't know yet."

"Maybe he likes you."

"I'm not his type. Too bony and freckly and red-haired. Not exactly the seventh-grade fashion statement."

"You don't know what his type is." Daisy G. grabbed Blister's chin and shook it. "You're a pretty girl, Alyssa

Reed, and you should know that. Stop thinking of yourself as a little wildcat with a mop of red hair and freckles and a skinny body and caterpillar legs — that's what you used to say about your legs." She took the lemon meringue out of the fridge. "Don't jump to conclusions, chicken soup. I can tell you're in the process of turning into a beauty."

"Like Raggedy Ann," Blister said, distracted.

She was thinking of a conversation she wanted to have with Daisy G: things she wanted to tell her, things she couldn't say to her mother, who was too easily upset, or her father, who used up all his sympathy with Tamara.

"You're the only one in the family who's always the same person, day after day," she told Daisy G.

Blister looked up from her plate, catching Daisy G.'s familiar sweet expression — her tiny bow lips painted with cherry-red lipstick, her head cocked to one side, her brown eyes soft with affection.

She wanted to tell Daisy G. about Jonah's missed kiss without telling her about Jonah, but she couldn't think of a way to do it.

Maybe in the morning before Daisy G. drove her home.

After dinner and the dishes and two pieces of lemon meringue pie with milky coffee, which Daisy G. allowed her to drink, Blister went upstairs to her room. There were three bedrooms on the second floor. One was Daisy G.'s, which had a big bed with a fluffy canopy and copies of Degas's dancer pictures hanging in black frames on the wall. Another was used as the living room, where her grandmother had put the furniture from downstairs when she designed the dance studio. And the last room belonged to Blister. It was where she had slept whenever she spent the night — a tiny room her grandmother had painted sunny yellow with a quilt on the bed and photographs of Blister hanging on the wall from the age of one day old to this year when she was thirteen. There was something reassuring about her childhood surrounding her, as if the accumulation of her own familiar face reinforced her sense of existence.

"Sleep tight and don't let the bedbugs bite," Daisy G. called from her room, the same line she had always used with Blister, the same girlish giggle after she spoke.

Blister crawled in between the sheets, snuggled into

the small depression in the mattress made by her own body, and lying in the cool bath of moonlight, she waited to fall asleep.

She tried to think happy thoughts as Daisy G. had told her to do, to think about Christmas and baking pies and shopping with her mother and being with Jonah when they were only best friends.

But each time she tried to think of happy times, an image of Jonah Morrison in the supply closet would crowd them out of her head. She couldn't sleep.

Her mind was running on a hamster wheel, around and around, and the moon seemed to get brighter, the room colder, the rattles in the old farmhouse louder, and finally Blister got out of bed and tiptoed to Daisy G.'s room.

Her grandmother slept on her back with the door open and she snored, which is what she was doing when Blister stopped at her door and waited.

"Daisy G.?"

"Yes, yes, I'm right here, wide-awake and snoring."

She turned on the light beside her bed and sat up.

"I can't sleep," Blister said.

Daisy G. gave a long, slow yawn, stretching her arms above her head.

"You need to be a dancer so your body is moving and moving all the time and your brain doesn't have a chance to get in your way."

She patted the other side of the double bed.

"Climb in with me."

Blister pulled down the covers on the other side of the bed and crawled in.

"So tell me your worry and we'll fix it."

"I have these troubles with men."

"Troubles with men?" Daisy G. asked, sitting up and turning on the light. "You didn't tell me you had boyfriends."

"I don't have boyfriends."

Blister put a pillow behind her back.

"I mean men like Dad."

"Of course you have trouble with him. He's a juvenile delinquent."

"And then there's Frank."

"Frank is not your problem."

"Except I live with him."

She buttoned and unbuttoned the top of her pajamas, thinking how much she should tell Daisy G. and whether she would understand.

"Most of the time, I can't stand Frank Holt and all of a sudden today, I started to like him."

"Good," Daisy G. said in her definite way. "I'm happy to hear that. Things change. That can be a good thing."

"I was sitting in the truck and Frank was driving and when I looked at him, I decided I was beginning to like him and now I feel disloyal to my father."

"It is a dilemma, sweetheart, but it's not your dilemma and there's nothing you can do about these men except '*Pack up your troubles in an old kit bag and smile, smile, smile,*'" Daisy G. sang out.

"That doesn't make sense."

"You can't change Frank or your dad, so hop aboard the happiness train and leave them in the dust."

"What about Jakob Cutter? Should I give back the rose?"

"Oh no, Alyssa, not the rose. You should keep the rose. Is it pink?"

"Red."

"Of course you should keep it. A crimson-red rose. Or is it bloodred?"

"Just red red."

"Keep it! What good is a rose to him?"

She reached over and turned off the light.

Blister slipped down under the covers, her head on the edge of the pillow, closing her eyes.

"Daisy G.?" she asked quietly.

"I'm right here beside you."

"Can I ask you one more thing?"

"Many things. As many as you like, sweet potato."

"About kissing."

"A very good subject, kissing."

"Do you remember how old you were the first time you were kissed?"

"The first time?" Daisy G. turned on her side, her head resting in her hand so her soft breath was warm on Blister's cheek. "Hmmmm. The first time was Sam Freemont and I was in the sixth grade and he had the worst breath I've ever smelled. Just thinking about him now, I can smell that awful breath."

"Was sixth grade early for a girl in your generation to kiss?"

"I'm sure it was no different for me and no different for your mother and no different for you. Times change but not girls."

"What happened to you?"

"Most of the girls in my class started to play kissing games with dirty-necked boys in the fifth grade. I thought that was disgusting so when Sam Freemont expressed an interest in kissing me one afternoon after school, I agreed but I wanted to do it in private."

"So did you?"

"I did. I was twelve years old then and didn't kiss another boy for a long time."

"How come so long?"

"Sam Freemont had very bad breath," Daisy G. said, pinching her nose. "How old were you at your first kiss?"

"Thirteen," Blister said, whispering it in the air and hoping it would get lost there. "Last week was the first time."

"Jonah?"

"He kissed me trying for my lips and missed them and then he kissed me on my chin."

"Now that's an entertaining development."

"It's a bad development."

"Why bad?"

"Because our friendship could die of it."

Blister turned over on her side, inching closer to her grandmother, the moonlight through the window sliding over her shoulder, painting Daisy G. silver.

"Already our friendship is in trouble," Blister said. "All Jonah does is hang on to the popular boys in seventh grade and they're disgusting."

"What do you *want* to happen?"

"*Nothing*," Blister said, closing her eyes, nestling her head against her grandmother's arm. "I want things to be exactly the way they've always been with Jonah."

"It's your choice," Daisy G. said.

"I want to be friends with Jonah. Real and perfect friends the way we were at Bixley."

"Tomorrow," Daisy G. said, "I'll make banana bread and hot chocolate and we'll talk in the daylight."

*　　*　　*

Sometime later, maybe much later, Blister finally fell asleep, the bed warm with bodies, the wind outside slapping the branches against the windowpane, Daisy G. snoring once again.

In the morning, the first thing Blister remembered was the living room of a dollhouse with red and yellow plastic furniture and red and yellow people, her father and Frank Holt and Jonah Morrison and Jakob Cutter floating through the room, and she was sitting on the mantelpiece over the fireplace, a fire blazing underneath.

She told it all to Daisy G.

"You made up that dream," Daisy G. said.

"Maybe I made it up," Blister said, licking the whipped cream off the top of her hot chocolate. "I can't remember."

Jack Reed used to say he was losing his grip. "Oh my gosh," he'd say, throwing up his hands. "I'm losing my grip."

Which was how Blister was beginning to feel, as if she were in the process of flying out of control if she didn't hold on tight.

10

The Invasion of Jakob Cutter

W hen Blister went to the market on Sunday afternoon to buy groceries for Jonah, Jakob Cutter was there. She was standing in the cereal aisle thinking of what to buy and suddenly there was Jakob standing next to her in sloppy black jeans hanging low on his bottom and a canvas jacket with NIGHT RIDER in red letters across the front.

She stared at the lineup of cereals without looking at him, as if his arrival in her private life was of no consequence.

"Did you get my present?" he asked casually, resting his elbow on the cereal shelf.

"I got it," Blister said, her heart beating in her throat.

She took a box of Cheerios off the shelf and put it in her cart.

"So what do you hear from Jonah?" he asked.

"Nothing."

She pushed her cart down the aisle to the peanut butter and jelly and took jars of strawberry jelly and chunky peanut butter.

"He's your best friend. He ought to be in touch," he said with a smirk in his voice.

She shook her head.

"The police came to my house today," Jakob said. "I was watching TV and they came up to the front porch and knocked on the door."

She was pretending to read the ingredients on the back label of the chunky peanut butter.

"Yeah," he said. "A squad car with two policemen pulled up and got out and walked up our front steps keeping their hands on their guns like I was dangerous or something."

He checked her response.

"They knew that I'd been at the bus station where Jonah was caught on Friday night."

Blister took a box of maple granola bars off the shelf, opened the carton, took one out, and dropped the box in the cart.

Jakob reached in to take a granola bar for himself.

"Okay?" he asked.

She didn't reply.

"So," he went on. "My mom let them in the house and then she got me up from the TV and we all sat around the kitchen table and they asked me questions about Jonah and I said I hadn't seen him since Friday night at the bus station and they asked did I know about the electronic equipment and I said I read about it in the paper."

Blister turned.

"But that's not true. You knew what happened before it was in the paper."

"It IS true," Jakob said, sticking his hands in his pockets, following Blister down the aisle. "The police came to my house because Jonah has disappeared and they're looking for him and thought I might know where he is."

Blister took a loaf of whole wheat bread off the shelf.

"Did you know he'd disappeared?" Jakob asked.

Blister's cheeks were burning.

"His mother filed a missing-child report yesterday," he said.

She wheeled her cart to the end of the aisle and stopped at the crackers, taking Wheat Thins off the shelf.

"Are you going to talk or not?" he asked. "Did Ms. Morrison call you about Jonah bolting?"

Maybe she should get cookies, she was thinking, thin butter cookies in a slender box. But knowing Jonah, he'd probably eat them all at once.

"We're friends, you and me, right? I'm just keeping you up-to-date since Jonah is your very best friend in the world. You said that yourself."

"You and I are NOT friends," Blister said, turning right and down the condiments aisle. "We're not even beginning to be friends."

"I think you're reasonably cool, so who knows? We could end up being pretty much inseparable, you living across the street and stuff."

This remark pleased him. He laughed hard, tears

running down his cheeks, leaning against the bakery goods shelf. He took a pencil out of his pocket and slipped it behind his ear.

"So what're you up to this afternoon?"

"I'm busy."

"If you'd like to come over and watch some TV and order pizza, my parents are going to the movies and I've got to babysit my little brother."

"I can't," Blister said.

"How come?"

"It's Sunday night and we have a family rule to spend it together," Blister said.

It wasn't a family rule. There had never been any family rules in the Reed family.

"We hold on to life with our fingertips," Daisy G. would say.

No rules now or ever, even before her parents were divorced.

"You have rules?" Jakob asked.

Blister took a jar of cranberry-apple juice off the shelf, some gingersnaps, dried apricots, and a package of gummy bears.

"Not in my family," Jakob said. "My mom trusts me. So does my dad."

Blister got in line to check out.

"I don't know *why* they trust you," she said. "I wouldn't."

His lips turned up in a wicked smile and he laughed again, slapping the checkout counter so the cashier gave him a "beat it, kiddo" look.

"They trust me because I'm t-r-u-s-t-w-o-r-t-h-y."

He slipped into the line behind her, resting his hand on the handles of the cart.

"You're so weird," he said, leaning slightly against her, enough to make her step away.

She lined up her purchases on the counter.

"Trust me. I've had a lot of girlfriends, about nine of them since fifth grade, and you're not like any other girl at Memorial. At least not the ones I know."

He leaned over the grocery cart so his stomach was balancing like a seesaw on the handlebar and his head was upside down in the cart.

"I don't get you," he said from that position. "But you look better upside down."

Blister paid the cashier, picked up her two paper bags, and headed out of the store, Jakob behind her.

"Next time you come here, leave your boyfriend behind, okay?" the cashier called after her.

"He's not my boyfriend," Blister said, waiting for the automatic doors to open.

"Jonah's in a lot of trouble," Jakob was saying, as they exited. "Shoplifting is a big deal, in case you didn't know."

"He didn't shoplift."

"You already said that yesterday."

"I haven't changed my mind," Blister said.

He kept in step with her fast pace.

Blister headed up the street toward Bixley Elementary, Jakob beside her. Two more blocks and she'd be there and so would Jakob if he continued to walk along beside her and Jonah would be waiting behind the back door for Blister to come with the groceries. She couldn't exactly stop at Bixley with a load of groceries for Jonah Morrison with Jakob at her side. So she walked home.

The house would be empty. Her mother was at the movies with Frank, but she would have left a key under the doormat of the new house the way she did when they lived in the apartment.

There was nothing she could do about Jonah. He'd just have to believe that eventually she would come. She had never let him down.

"What're you going to do for the rest of the afternoon?" Jakob asked.

"I'm going home to fix up my new room and then my grandmother is coming over for dinner."

"Boring."

Jakob was staring at her and she could feel her face turning red. Probably she was blushing.

She wasn't exactly afraid of Jakob Cutter, but she didn't want him in the empty house with her. Whatever his parents thought about him, they were his parents, but Blister knew he wasn't trustworthy. There was something out of bounds and intrusive about him that bothered Blister, and she hated the way he kept looking at her out of the corner of his eye.

"How come you're staring at me like that?" she finally asked.

"To see what you look like. What else?"

"You can see without trying so hard," she said.

They had come to Acorn Street, turning left off the main avenue, and it was beginning to rain, the sky suddenly dark, the air misty. She picked up her pace.

At the house, she put down the groceries and checked under the mat for the key to the front door.

"Remember I told you someone died in your house?"

"The grandmother. Frank told me."

"Frank, the mover guy."

"Frank, my mother's boyfriend."

"And it doesn't weird you out to have someone die in your new house?"

"People have to die someplace," Blister said, giving him a chilly look.

Her stomach was queasy, her heart banging as if her chest were an empty tin can.

"So can I come in?" Jakob asked as she put the key in the lock.

"Nope," she said. "I'm not allowed to have strangers in. Even the ones I already know, like you."

The front door opened easily.

"Just how old are you?" he asked, leaning against the front door, his eyebrows raised, his lips curling up, one side a little higher than the other. "Five?"

"Same as you."

"I'm fourteen," he said. "Held back in sixth grade for incorrigible behavior."

"I'm thirteen."

"And you're still not old enough to decide who comes in your house without your parent's permission?"

"Nope."

Blister pushed open the door and had just stepped inside when Jakob pressed in behind her.

"So." He walked into the living room and sat down on the couch.

"I'm in your house and I'm sitting down in the living room with my feet on the coffee table." He put his feet up on the unpacked book boxes. "And I'm staying here until I'm ready to leave."

She took the groceries to the kitchen, set them down beside the fridge, and sat down, out of breath. Maybe, she thought, she was having a heart attack. Was that possible at thirteen? She had just raised her arms up over her head to catch her breath when the telephone rang.

It was Jonah.

"I'm in the principal's office and I called information and they gave me your new number."

He was near tears.

"I waited and waited," he said. "And you didn't come and you always do what you say so I thought something had happened."

"Stuff came up."

"Like an accident?"

"Family things."

She had turned facing the hall so she could see Jakob sitting on the couch in the living room, his feet on the boxes, his back to her.

"I've got the groceries for you and I'll see you at five, same place we planned to meet," she said quickly. "And don't worry if I'm a little late." Then she hung up the phone.

Jakob was slouched on the couch, his legs crossed at the ankles.

Blister opened the front door.

"So good-bye, Jakob. You've got to go now."

He got up from the couch, stretching so his shirt came up, showing his belly.

"Good idea. Thanks for the invite. I got stuff to do and can't hang around here any longer," he went on as if it had been his decision to leave.

At the front door, he stopped and, in a gesture too swift for Blister to see, he took the pencil from behind his ear and put it between her parted lips.

"Smoke?" he asked, and then jumping down the front steps, he ran across the street.

11

In the Dark

blister lay on her back, her head resting on a package of soft toilet paper, her arms loose beside her. There were no lights in the supply closet and with the door shut the room was dark.

Her mind was spinning with worries she'd never had. It was as if she were stopped at the top of a Ferris wheel, the chair swinging back and forth, with a sense of falling although the safety rail was locked across her belly.

She wished she were little, back at the house in the country where they used to live with her mother and father and Me and Ow, her father's old cats, sleeping at the end of her bed. Her life had been simple then. She had known what to expect every day, knew who her friends were and her parents' friends, knew her mother and father and usually Daisy G. would be home for dinner every night.

Since then, everything had changed. The days were full of surprises. Blister was even a surprise to herself. One moment she was her old familiar cheerful self and the next moment, out of nowhere, a dark mood crawled into her head.

Something was going on that she didn't understand.

"Tell me about Jakob again," Jonah said.

"I told you everything."

"So you think he framed me?"

"I don't know, Jonah. I just don't know. But if you're telling the truth, someone did."

"What exactly does it mean to *frame* me?" Jonah asked.

"Someone made it look as if you'd shoplifted."

"And you think that person was Jakob Cutter?"

"I think it could be."

"Him or Monster Bar. I never did like Monster Bar." Jonah turned on his side so the warm air of his breath blew across her face.

"Do you know Jakob?" Jonah asked.

"I know who he is."

"Yeah, who doesn't? But you're not friends, right?"

"We're not friends," Blister said, a twinge in her stomach when she said it. She had not told Jonah that Jakob lived across the street from her new house. She knew he wouldn't be glad to hear about it. It wasn't exactly lying, she thought, but it was like lying and she was not a liar.

"I wish we had music in here, don't you?" Jonah said.

"Like the radio?"

"Like any music. Maybe Jeannie Forever."

"I don't like Jeannie Forever," Blister said. "She has a whiny voice."

"I like her whiny songs. They're sort of romantic."

"Whatever that means."

She had heard something and was listening to hear if anyone was in the school on a Sunday night who might open the door to the supply closet and find them.

"Why are you so quiet?" Jonah rested his head on his fist, his elbow poking her stomach. She could just barely make out the definition of his face in the dark.

"Someone could be here."

"On Sunday night? Not a chance."

But Blister was sure she had heard something.

"I'm thinking you should go home tonight when my mom comes to pick me up. She can take you back to your apartment."

"I like it here."

"Not when school opens tomorrow, you won't," Blister said. "Tomorrow you'll hate it."

He was watching her. She could feel him move closer and it made her uneasy. But she didn't turn her face toward him, and kept very still, waiting for something to happen.

The air in the closet was hot and close and she wanted to throw open the door, air out the space.

"I wanted to hang out with guys like Jakob because people take notice of them," Jonah was saying. "Everyone knows who Jakob Cutter is and I wanted to be like him."

"That's a stupid wish," Blister said. "Jakob's a creep."

"You know what else?" Jonah said.

"Don't tell me. It'll make me mad."

"When I saw the story in the newspaper Saturday morning about the kid who shoplifts and I knew that kid was me, I was excited. Did you see it in the paper?"

"You know I saw it."

"I was thinking about Thomas Hale sitting in his kitchen wherever he lives with a beer and a roast beef on rye like he loves to eat and he's opening the newspaper and reading that story about me and thinking, 'That's Jonah Morrison, my boy, and he got himself a mention in the newspaper.'"

"Why would Thomas Hale be impressed with shoplifting?"

"He'd be impressed that I was in the newspaper. Thomas likes those things. He thinks they're important."

"Anyway, he doesn't live here. I think you told me he lives in Boston and he wouldn't be reading the newspaper from New Haven or North Haven or anyplace else except Boston, right?"

"But if he did, he'd probably know it was me."

"You DIDN'T shoplift."

"Right. I didn't."

"You drive me crazy, Jonah Morrison," Blister said, scrunching down in the darkness.

Outside the door, it sounded as if something had fallen over, a thump, followed by the sound of footsteps.

"What happens if someone opens the door?" Blister whispered.

"Quiet." Jonah inched away from Blister into a corner of the closet, slipping along the floor. "Follow me. Just feel where I'm going into the back, behind the books."

Blister followed on her hands and knees until they were pressed into a corner of the closet.

They could hear voices. It sounded like two people talking quietly and one was laughing. Then the door opened and a shaft of light slid above them.

"This is the supply closet."

It was a woman's voice, vaguely familiar, maybe Ms. Bralove.

"We keep everything here — graham crackers and paper towels and books and art supplies. Anything you need."

"Do the students know what the plans are for next week?" It was another woman's voice, but younger.

"I've left you all the details for Monday, Tuesday, and Wednesday while I'm gone," the first one said. "They're pretty good kids. You shouldn't have any trouble."

And the door shut.

Jonah and Blister were silent. They could hear the footsteps diminishing, the voices disappearing, and then they heard nothing at all.

"Whew!" Jonah dropped his head on Blister's shoulder.

"It's going to be hard for you to stay hidden at school on Monday," Blister said. "Think about it, Jonah. One way or another, you're going to have to go home, so you might as well do it now unless you plan to die here."

"I don't plan to die here."

"Then I'll make plans for you," Blister said. "You'll come with me now and we'll go out to dinner with my mom and Frank and then we'll go to your house."

They were sitting up, leaning against the wall.

"You better make up your mind about going home now because I have to go at six," Blister said.

They sat in silence waiting, Jonah checking his watch, time moving as slow as a caterpillar toward six o'clock.

"Blister?" Jonah said finally.

Her eyes were closed, her head pressed against the wall, and she was thinking about nothing at all. She felt as if Jonah and Jakob and her father and Frank were trapped in a spiderweb inside her brain and she wanted to dust them out, leave them on the floor of the supply closet, and shut the door behind her.

"You know what?"

"What?" Blister replied.

"I was thinking that I don't feel the same way I used to feel about you," Jonah said quietly.

Blister pulled her knees under her chin and wrapped her arms around them.

"I feel better," he said. "I'm sort of lonely about you."

"Here I am, so you don't need to be lonely."

"I think I love you but not the same way as I used to," Jonah said. "You know what I mean?"

Blister flung her arm across her face so she couldn't see even the shadow of Jonah beside her. She knew what he was trying to say to her but she didn't want to hear it. It was so like Jonah to talk around the corners of a subject like that, awkward and sweet and even sort of foolish.

"Well?"

She rested her chin on her knees.

"I don't know *what* to say," she said.

"Tell me that we're boyfriend and girlfriend. Boyfriend and girlfriend forever. That's all you have to say."

"We're only thirteen."

"So?" Jonah asked.

"Thirteen's too young for forever."

"Just say for *a while* and we'll see what happens."

Blister put her head down on her knees, a large lump forming in her throat the size of a tennis ball. She didn't know what she thought about anything any longer except math class. She hated math class. And she hated that her small, sensible world was exploding in a thousand tiny bits that would take months to put back together so they fit.

"I can't be your girlfriend now, Jonah."

"Not ever?"

"Not now," Blister said.

Jonah fell silent, considering.

"Okay," he said finally, taking a deep breath and then, as if Blister had promised him everything he had ever wanted for the rest of his life, he added, "That's good. That's very fine and I'll just wait until NOW is over."

12
Triangle

blister sat behind Daisy G. watching the twirls of her wiry hair bounce up and down over the high seat as the truck bumped along the road on their way home, watching Frank Holt out of the corner of her eye. She liked the way his black beard spread across his chin, his large hairy arms tensed on the steering wheel, his eyes in the rearview mirror set deep in his head. She was beginning to like him. Just the size of him was comforting.

"Absolutely no luck finding Jonah?" Frank asked.

"None," Blister said. "Did Mom speak to Ms. Morrison?"

"She did."

"And Ms. Morrison hasn't heard from him?"

"She hasn't, but she thinks he'd come home if somehow he wasn't afraid of what would happen with the police."

"Like what?"

"He has been charged with shoplifting and has to appear before a judge," Frank said.

"I thought he had already been arrested and the police took him to the precinct Friday night and Ms. Morrison picked him up."

"That's right," Frank said. "He was released into her custody, but he doesn't know the consequences until he appears before a judge."

"So what can we do?"

"Ms. Morrison believes Jonah would come home if the real shoplifters would come forward and confess."

"They won't."

"And you're still convinced that Jonah didn't do it?"

"Completely sure," Blister said.

"Of course he didn't," Daisy G. said. "And I'm going to make Jonah a Strawberry Surprise as soon as he comes home."

"The trouble is there's no way to prove he didn't do it," Blister said.

"Only his word against the facts," Frank Holt said.

"But there were witnesses," Blister said. "Jakob Cutter and Monster Bar and Eddie James were witnesses."

Frank turned down the Top 40 on the radio.

"You could help, Blister."

"I'm not going to talk to Jakob, if that's what you mean," she said. "We aren't friends."

"You can change that," Frank said.

"I don't want to."

"Jakob's a braggart," Frank said. "You're clever enough to get him to tell you about Friday night and he won't even know what he's doing."

"How do I do that?"

"He's a boaster, full of self-admiration. Let him know you think Jonah Morrison is cool."

"Jonah's completely uncool," Blister said. "That's why I like him."

Frank pulled up to the curb in front of the new house and turned off the engine.

"I'm suggesting you make up a story," Frank said. "Like pretend to be in love with Jonah."

"I can't pretend that," Blister said. "I'm not in love with him."

*   *   *

Mary Reed had made spaghetti and real meatballs and hot garlic bread and they sat in the kitchen surrounded by packed boxes, eating by candlelight on paper plates.

It was early — just dark — and beyond the large kitchen window, the backyard glittered as if shards of moonlight were sprinkled on the grass.

Blister twirled the long strands of spaghetti around her fork, nearly too exhausted to sit up.

Frank opened a bottle of red wine, pouring a small amount for Blister. Then he turned on the radio to the all-music station.

"To our new lives together," he said, raising his glass, and Blister raised her glass in concert, drinking the wine in a single swallow.

Frank took Mary Reed's hand and asked her to dance

and they danced around the kitchen table, and then Frank put his hand out to Daisy G.

"I dance alone, Frank Holt," she said with a bow of her head. "I haven't danced with a man for over twenty years."

"Blister?" he asked.

"Tomorrow," Blister said automatically, and if she hadn't been so weary, she might have added, "This is TOO weird! My own parents NEVER danced at home and they were MARRIED."

But she didn't and Frank sat back down at the table and poured himself another half glass of wine.

Later, upstairs in her new bedroom, her light off, and Bewilder, smelling vaguely of skunk, asleep at the bottom of her bed, Blister looked out at the Cutter house.

The lights were on, the television shimmering in the living room, casting its electronic reflection on the wall. On the front porch, Blister could barely make out the outline of Jakob Cutter sitting on the railing, the glow of an iPod marking a tiny light circle in the black space above his lap.

She sat on her bed for a long time watching him. From time to time he bounced a basketball with one hand while he was lying on the railing. Then there'd be another flash of light from a match and another tiny circle hanging in the air bright enough to see from across the street.

Downstairs she could hear the *slap-slap-slap* of bare feet on the hardwood floor. The illuminated alarm clock on her dresser read 11:15 and she was still awake.

"Baby!" Frank was calling out loud enough to be heard in Blister's room on the third floor. "Where are you?"

She heard her mother's high giggle.

Daisy G. was singing the same refrain again and again, pretending to be different instruments, the high strings of a violin, the trill of piano keys, the low boom of the bass.

"Daisy G.?" Frank called. "You're hurting my ears."

No one had come upstairs to tell Blister good night. It was as if she didn't even live in the new house with them. As if she were back in the old apartment and they had neglected to pack her up with the books and china.

Her eyes filled with tears. That was the difference

with thirteen, she was thinking. When she was twelve, she would never have wasted her time crying in the dark.

Tomorrow was Monday and she hadn't done her homework. She couldn't even remember where she'd put her books when she emptied out her backpack to fill it with groceries for Jonah.

First period was health education and there was never homework. Blister usually slept through Ms. Knickerbocher with her tiny bluebird voice standing at the blackboard drawing body parts. Tomorrow would be the second showing of *The Romance of Jason and Elise* to the seventh-grade girls during gym class, as if the first showing hadn't been sufficient.

Jason and Elise were stick figures with round heads and straight lines for arms and legs, as if they had been drawn by a child. Elise had a triangle of skirt and Jason had stick-up hair and big shoes, but otherwise they looked exactly the same, with round eyes and small ears and turned-up lips.

The film was about the necessary protection for girls to use with boys, the dos and don'ts, with explicit

descriptions of the efficient way the body works for repro-
duction.

"Smart sex," as Ms. Knickerbocher described it.

Nothing about romance. Nothing about a girl and
boy together in a dark room with music playing.

No wonder so many people got divorced if the only
information anyone had about getting married came from
The Romance of Jason and Elise in health education.

She rolled over on her stomach.

The night had gotten cold. She could feel the chill
behind the windowpanes of the skylight above her and from
the line of windows behind her bed. She scrunched down to
the middle of the bed, wrapping the covers around her.

When Daisy G. came in, she had inched her way
down under the covers. Not even her head showed above
the comforter.

"Alyssa?"

"I'm wide-awake," Blister said, pulling her feet up to
make room for her grandmother to sit down on the side
of the bed and stretch out her legs.

"A problem a day keeps the doctor away."

"Which problem do you mean?"

"The Jakob Cutter problem."

"Oh, that."

"He called earlier and wants to walk to school with you tomorrow. He said he'd be here at seven-thirty."

"I'm planning to be sick tomorrow." Blister sat up and leaned against the headboard, pulling her legs up under her chin. "I feel it coming on."

"I think you should be careful. No good deed goes unpunished."

Blister burrowed her head in her knees.

"I want to change schools. That's what I've been thinking. A girl at Memorial told me that Acorn Street is the dividing line between Memorial and Samuel Taylor Junior High and I'd like to switch to Samuel Taylor."

"Nothing will change just by changing schools," Daisy G. said. "You'll be the same girl in a different location and there'll be another boy like Jonah and a creep like Jakob. It's no good, sweetheart. You carry your troubles inside."

"There'll never be another boy like Jonah," Blister

said sadly. "I just want him to be the old Jonah and not the new one."

"Then tell him that," Daisy G. said. "And *smile, smile, smile*."

"Don't sing, Daisy G., please. It makes me twitchy."

"Such a dilemma to be a girl in seventh grade," Daisy G. said. "Either too many boys putting pressure on you or too few of them. Never the right mix. It was like that when I was a girl longing for boyfriends and having none at all."

"I don't want a boyfriend," Blister said. "I want everything to be normal."

"This is normal."

"Then I want it to be something else."

Daisy G. brushed her hand across Blister's face, the way she used to do when she was small.

"Too much going on for such a slip of a girl."

"Even with Frank."

"What about Frank?"

"It's like I'm standing barefoot in a cold water puddle that's suddenly turning warm."

Tonight on the drive from the Morrisons' apartment to the house on Acorn Street, Blister had glanced over at Frank and what she felt was a rush of affection for him.

Since dinner when she watched him dance with her mother, Blister had been thinking about Frank Holt, thinking what a strong, kind man he was, how she sometimes wished he were her real father and Jack Reed was someone else, maybe an uncle or a second cousin. Not gone from her life, but another kind of relative.

"I'm beginning to like Frank," she said.

"Things could be worse than liking Frank Holt," Daisy G. said.

"What about Dad?"

Jack Reed made Blister angry. He promised this and that and forgot what he'd promised, forgot his money, forgot to be on time to pick her up, even forgot her birthday once.

And Tamara, with all her demands and temper tantrums and whiny afternoons sitting in a blue funk on the couch in the living room of Jack Reed's apartment with her stupid French poodle on her lap.

"Frank's not your father," Daisy G. said. "He'll never be your father."

"I can still feel bad about it."

"Of course you can. You can feel any way you like."

Daisy G. was holding on to one of the bedposts as a ballet barre and doing a high kick.

"There are just too many men in your life. No wonder you're upset." She leaned over and kissed the top of Blister's head. *"Whenever I feel afraid, I hold my head erect, and whistle a happy tune, so no one will suspect I'm afraid,"* she sang.

"I'm not afraid, Daisy G.," Blister said. "I'm bothered."

"Bewitched, bothered, and bewildered."

"Daisy G.!"

Blister put a pillow over her head and pressed it against her ears so she could barely hear Daisy G. singing as she went down the steps.

"Good night, sweetheart, now it's time to go . . ."

Later, unable to sleep, the house silent, her head throbbing, Blister got out of bed, turned on the light, and opened her suitcase.

At the bottom was a short, short skirt she had borrowed a long time ago from Tamara, a fitted blue turtleneck sweater, and striped tights. In the pocket of the suitcase, she found her makeup kit with lavender blush and eye shadow. She took off her pajamas and tried on clothes, brushing her cheeks with blush, her eyes with smoky blue eye shadow. She found some mascara of her mother's she had taken from the medicine cabinet in the old apartment.

It was after midnight. She set the alarm for six and, suddenly overcome by sleep, too tired to get back in her pajamas, to wash her face, to take off her makeup, she climbed into bed in her clothes, turned out the light, pulled up the covers, and fell immediately to sleep.

13

White Lies and Strawberry Surprise

the silver light from a full moon came through the skylight, splashing over her bed and waking Blister. Three A.M. registered on the illuminated alarm clock. She threw off the covers, forgetting that she'd gone to bed in the hand-me-down skirt from Tamara and the tiny tight turtleneck. She was wide awake.

On the landing between the second and third floors, Bewilder, curled into a half-circle, lay on her back. She lifted her head as Blister walked by and followed her downstairs. Something about a living creature, even bad-smelling Bewilder, lifted Blister's spirits, and she picked the cat up and kissed the top of her musty, matted head. The door to her mother's room was shut and the room was silent. Daisy G. was snoring down the hall in the guest room where the Cranes' grandmother had died, her breath catching in a high whistle.

In the kitchen, she put Bewilder on the table, opened the fridge, and took out a half gallon of milk, pouring a bowl for the cat and a cup in a saucepan to heat for herself. Daisy G. made hot milk for Blister when she couldn't sleep and though it never seemed to work, she loved the warm, sweet taste of it.

She sat, tucking her legs underneath her, her elbow on the table, her chin in her hand. Bewilder was batting her nose with a yellow paw, rubbing her head against Blister's chin, purring the loud, honking purr of an old cat.

A plan was forming in her mind. She could feel it developing like a Polaroid photograph rising from a muddy surface. But she couldn't see it yet. She simply knew some kind of plan was on its way to her.

Ever since the summer when Frank Holt arrived by surprise and school began at Memorial Junior High and Jonah deserted her, Blister had been in the gradual process of slipping away from herself, something that had never happened to her, even in the worst weeks after Lila Rose was born dead. It was as if she was in a heavy current floating downstream, and she couldn't catch up to her own disappearing body.

The kitchen was luminous and mysterious in the moonlight, and she sat very still, watching the light sprinkling her arms and legs with silver glitter.

She was beginning to feel like herself, her old familiar self — what Daisy G. would call by the phrases she rattled off like popular songs — the "look-on-the-bright-side girl," the "pull-yourself-up-by-your-bootstraps girl," the "don't-cry-over-spilled-milk girl," "the best-defense-is-a-good-offense girl."

She made toast with homemade raspberry jam and peeled a banana, watching the minute hand on the kitchen clock jump to four A.M.

She was up for the day.

At seven-thirty, Jakob Cutter would arrive to walk to school with her. Sometime, maybe during fourth-period study hall or after lunch, she would go to Bixley Elementary. Jonah had told her before she left on Sunday

166

night that he'd found a place to hide during the day under the stage in the assembly room.

Perhaps her instincts were wrong, she thought, although she had always trusted them in the past. Perhaps Jonah HAD shoplifted to prove that he was one of the gang.

Somehow soon she had to find a way to force or persuade Jakob Cutter to tell the truth about what had happened at the bus station.

She heard the morning paper slap the wood of the front porch and opened the door to get it, sitting on the bottom step of the stairs to read it. Skipping the first section of national news, she turned to the Metro section and read the headlines.

Accident on Parkway Kills One

Plans for the Construction of

New Elementary School Approved

Mayor of New Haven Undergoes Triple Bypass

And then on page two, top right:

Memorial Junior High Student, Accused of Shoplifting,

Reported Missing

The article was very short.

The Memorial Junior High School student, accused of shoplifting electronic equipment Friday night was reported missing by his family on Saturday afternoon. According to a family member, the student disappeared from his home that morning, leaving a note that said he was "gone for good."

Upstairs, she heard Daisy G. getting out of bed, her door open, her bare knobby feet slapping down the steps.

"Good morning, rosedrop," she said, kissing Blister on the top of the head. "Early for you to be having breakfast."

"Early for you too."

Blister folded the newspaper and put it on a chair. She didn't want to talk about Jonah while her mind was in the process of resolving itself to a plan of action.

"It's so bright for the middle of the night that I woke up with a start and thought to myself, 'I'm going to make Jonah a Strawberry Surprise and then he'll come out of hiding like a homing pigeon sniffing Strawberry Surprise in his future.'"

"Yum. He'll love that."

"I got the strawberries and whipped cream and angel food cake yesterday so I'll put it all together — except for the whipped-cream icing hiding the strawberries — and stick it in the fridge, and I bet you thunder, Jonah will be home by tonight."

Daisy G. took the premade angel food cake out of the cupboard and put it on the table.

"The cat's got to leave the kitchen. I don't want to make Cat Hair Surprise."

"I'll take her upstairs."

Blister lifted Bewilder, putting the old cat around her shoulders the way Frank carried her.

"Back to bed?" Daisy G. asked.

"Maybe," she said, although she had no intention of going back to bed.

"Remember, that boy you despise is coming to walk to school with you about seven o'clock."

"I won't forget."

Upstairs, Blister stood in front of the full-length mirror on the back of her closet door and tried on the clothes in her suitcase. The short, short skirt she'd slept in was

169

too wrinkled. She tried on a pencil-thin khaki skirt that hung on her hips like a sackcloth and black jeans with a turquoise-studded belt that her father had brought her from his honeymoon with Tamara in New Mexico. She liked turtlenecks best because of her scrawny neck, but she loved the feel on her skin of the loose Indian-print shirts, very thin and silky, which Tamara had given her for her birthday. She wanted to wear boots, the kind her mother wore, black leather, which came up to her knee. Perhaps she'd borrow Mary Reed's.

Looking out the window at the Cutters' house, she saw Ms. Cutter standing next to a lamp in the living room window rocking the baby. The rest of the house was dark. She wondered which room was Jakob's and whether he was in the upstairs room with the light on and whether he ever had trouble sleeping.

The black jeans looked best, she decided, along with a red turtleneck sweater Daisy G. had given her for Christmas, and her mother's boots with the pants legs tucked in so she looked like a jockey.

The red turtleneck with her red hair made her face —

even with freckles splashed across her brow — too pale, so she brushed some more blue eye shadow on her eyelids, rose blush high on her cheeks, and gold glitter across her nose and brow.

It was a good look, she thought. Sassy without being stupid about it.

"Stupid," according to Daisy G., was when a girl dressed in thin tops so her nipples showed, or too-tight skirts, or wore brown lipstick or silver studs in her lips, or dyed her hair purple.

"It may be true that you can't judge a book by its cover," Daisy G. had told Blister just last summer. "But the cover tells you something about the book and don't ever pretend it doesn't."

She found her backpack under the bed, sat down at the desk, took out her math and language arts and social studies books, and by seven o'clock when the doorbell rang she had finished all the homework she had failed to get done over the weekend. She was a good student. Not a brilliant student and not an average C/C-student either. But she had to work at it. She could easily fail math or Spanish or even biology if she didn't study.

When Blister came downstairs, Jakob Cutter was in the kitchen sitting on one of the boxes, eating a chocolate doughnut.

"We're going to be late for school," Jakob said.

She sat down at the table and took a banana from the bowl of fruit.

"I think I'm getting strep throat," she said to Daisy G., who had put the Strawberry Surprise in the fridge and was making Morning Glory muffins.

Frank Holt was eating standing up.

"I got strep too," Jakob said, a half-smile on his face. "You must've given it to me yesterday."

"I don't think so," Blister said. "I wasn't anywhere near you and I'm not planning to be."

"Break my heart," Jakob said, bending in an exaggerated bow to Frank and Daisy G.

"Sayonara," he said, opening the back door. "We're off to the Memorial Junior High torture chamber."

Blister took a tuna sandwich her mother had made out of the fridge and stuffed it in her backpack, put the straps over her shoulders, and headed out the back door.

"Don't say 'Have a good day,'" Blister said to Frank.

"Don't worry. I never do." Frank smiled.

She walked just ahead of Jakob with her back straight, her shoulders up, her arms swinging, conscious of her gait.

"You look like a raccoon," Jakob said, huffing to keep up with her. "What's the blue stuff plastered on your eyelids?"

"It's called eye shadow, as you very well know," Blister said. "And I wear it because I admire the raccoon look."

Jakob laughed.

"You're not a pushover. I'll give you that," he said, pulling up his sloppy, beltless jeans hanging off his hips. "So I read about Jonah in the newspaper this morning. Did you see it?"

"I saw it."

"Pretty stupid of him to run away. He must be scared."

"He doesn't get scared," Blister said. "In sixth grade, he started a television show."

"*JONAH, THE WHALE.* I heard about it."

"Nobody who's scared starts a television show at twelve years old."

"He's a nerd, Blister. You've got to admit that."

They crossed the avenue, heading past the front of Bixley Elementary, walking side by side.

"He's smart and imaginative and I respect him."

"Love him?"

"Not your business."

"So you love him. Silence means yes."

Jakob put his hand on her shoulder, leaned toward her, and whispered in her ear.

"Oh Jonah, my beloved, I love you forever."

Blister pressed her elbow into Jakob's ribs and he yelped.

"Go to school alone," she said.

"I won't leave."

"I'm stopping here."

She sat down on the front steps of Bixley.

"I'm not walking to school with you," she said. "You're a jerk."

"I'm sorry. That was a mistake."

"You're a coward, Jakob. You gain power by humiliating other people."

"Try making sense, okay?"

"Jonah Morrison is so much braver than you will ever be," she said.

Across the street, Monster Bar and Eddie James were coming up Pleasant Avenue, headed in their direction.

When they saw Jakob, they crossed the street.

"So what's up?" Monster Bar asked, slapping Jakob on the shoulder.

"You know Blister Reed?" Jakob asked.

"Yeah," Eddie James said. "I know Blister from math class."

"She's a friend of Jonah Morrison's."

"He's on his way to jail," Eddie said.

"Juvenile detention," Monster Bar said.

Blister stood up and slung her backpack over her shoulder.

"Did you hear he was missing?" Eddie asked.

"Yeah," Jakob said. "I read it in the paper."

"He's just a nerdy kid who wears his pants too high and gets that orangey wax in his ears. Right, Jakob?"

Blister headed up the street toward Prospect, Jakob behind her.

"Hey Jake," someone yelled. "Are you a tag-along wimp?"

Blister didn't turn around, but she knew the voice belonged to Monster Bar.

At Memorial, she ran up the steps ahead of Jakob, through the door, heading past the assembly room, the chemistry and biology lab, and down the corridor where the seventh-grade lockers were. She turned the corner and went down the last aisle of lockers where her locker was located.

Jakob came up behind her, breathless.

"Give me a break."

She opened the locker, took her literature book out of her backpack, and locked her backpack in the locker.

"Talk to me," he said.

"I have nothing to say."

She walked ahead of him into homeroom. Then she put her book and papers on her desk and told Eloise O'Reilly at the desk next to hers that she had an emergency and might be a little late to homeroom.

Jakob was waiting outside homeroom.

"What is going on?" he asked.

"I have an emergency and I have to leave."

"I'm coming too."

"No, you're not coming," Blister said, taking off down the side stairs and out the back door, headed toward Bixley Elementary at a tear.

Suddenly she wanted to see Jonah. Some sense of urgency had come over her as if something could have happened to him during the night. She could feel it at a distance.

She ran down Prospect, across Hamilton, and all the way to the back entrance of Bixley Elementary.

The younger grades entered by the back door and they were pouring into the building, up the steps with their tiny backpacks. She walked in with them, knowing what route to take to avoid the principal's office and the receptionist, who would ask what Blister was doing at the wrong school on a school day.

She went through the heavy double doors of the assembly room and the room was empty. No assembly on Monday. So she walked down the sloping auditorium to the stage, up the steps, behind the curtain, around the back of the stage, and underneath where Jonah said he would be hiding.

It was completely dark, but she could tell he was there. She could smell him. He smelled like popcorn.

"Hi," she said, out of breath. "It's me."

There was no headroom under the stage, so the ceiling grazed her head when she walked upright.

Jonah was crouched in a corner. There was enough light coming through the floorboards for Blister to see him clearly. His arms were folded across his chest, his face was red, and his eyes were swollen as if he had been crying.

"You look just terrible."

He didn't answer.

"Are you okay?"

He stared at her, his eyes frozen in place.

"You look intense."

"I'm not intense," he said finally.

"Jonah, talk to me. What's going on?"

He opened the bag of raisins she'd given him the night before and ate them one at a time.

"You're something different than I saw yesterday," Blister said. "I can tell."

"I'm angry."

"At me?"

She got down on her knees beside him, leaning against the side of the stage.

"At you."

"How come?"

"I saw you with Jakob Cutter walking to school. You walked in front of Bixley just as I was looking out the window on my way to hide under here."

"I did," Blister said quietly, thinking there she had been on the steps of Bixley with those terrible boys and in a window above her, Jonah was watching.

"And while I was watching, Eddie James came up with Monster Bar and Jakob put his head right next to yours. He was probably kissing you, but I was too far away to tell."

"He didn't kiss me."

"But you just sat there as if it was perfectly normal to hang out with my enemies."

"I'll tell you what happened."

"I don't want to hear. That's all. I thought you were loyal."

He took a granola bar out of the paper bag.

"I thought you were loyal too, and then you dropped me flat," Blister said. "Now listen to me."

"I won't talk."

"I couldn't help it," Blister said. "Jakob lives across the street from my new house."

As soon as she said it, Blister knew it was a mistake.

The color drained from Jonah's face.

"Jakob Cutter lives across the street from your new house?"

"Give me a chance to say something."

"We are not friends, you and me."

"Jonah, please," she hurried on. "Daisy G.'s making Strawberry Surprise for you. She's taking it over to your apartment tonight."

Jonah's plump face had fallen as if it had sunk backwards into a large dimple on both cheeks.

"Leave me alone, Alyssa Reed. I don't want to see you anymore again ever."

14

The True Story

the police came just before lunch and asked for Blister.

At the time, when the bell for lunch rang, Blister was sitting at her desk, unable to concentrate and weak with sadness.

"Did anyone read this morning's paper?" Ms. Newton asked, picking up a copy of the paper on her desk.

No one raised a hand.

"Memorial Junior High student detained for shoplifting reported missing," she said from memory. "No one knew about this?" she asked.

"I knew about it," Eloise Murphy said.

"Me too," Sam Settle said.

"Jonah Morrison!" came a voice from the back of the class.

"Jonah Morrison."

"Jonah Morrison."

"Jonah Morrison."

Ms. Newton waved her hand.

"Lunch," she said. "Off you go."

Blister lingered. She went up to Ms. Newton's desk where she was grading papers.

"It wasn't Jonah who shoplifted," she said.

Ms. Newton looked up from her papers.

"Maybe it wasn't," she said. "But kids do have a way of knowing what other kids do."

"Sometimes they lie," Blister said.

She wasn't fond of Ms. Newton.

Jakob was waiting for her outside the classroom.

"The police are here looking for Jonah," he said. "They want to speak to you."

"Why me?" Blister asked.

"You're his friend."

"I am his friend," Blister said, walking in the direction of her locker, expecting Jakob to follow her, but he did not. She opened the locker, took out the tuna fish sandwich, and went down the back stairs to the lunchroom. Her knees were weak, her stomach queasy, and she wanted to call her mother.

"Police are looking for you," Monster Bar said, thumping down the stairs behind her.

"I know," Blister said.

"So aren't you going to the principal's office to see them?"

"They can find me," she said.

She walked along the corridor, uncertain of what to do or what to say, whether to tell the police that she knew where Jonah was or to leave school without waiting to talk to them.

She sat down beside Eloise and Vicky Sant and opened her lunch.

"What's up?" Eloise asked. "You look upset."

"I'm not," Blister said, unwrapping her sandwich, although she didn't feel like eating.

At the next table, Jakob was sitting with some of his

popular friends, including Monster Bar. Eddie James was nowhere in sight.

"Did you hear about Jonah Morrison?" Vicky Sant asked. "He's the one who shoplifted at the electronics store. It was in the paper on Saturday morning."

"I heard about it," Eloise said.

"Well, now he's missing."

"No kidding. Did you know about Jonah, Blister?" Eloise asked. "I thought you guys were friends."

"We are," Blister said, tears gathering in spite of herself. "The newspaper didn't say that Jonah was the one who shoplifted."

"They're not allowed to use the name of a juvenile," Vicky Sant said. "That's what my dad told me."

"Jonah doesn't seem the type of guy to shoplift," Eloise said. "Too nerdy."

"Every guy I know is the type," Vicky Sant said, spilling potato chips out of the bag to pass around.

The loudspeaker interrupted conversations when it blasted through the lunchroom, the raspy voice of the principal, Ms. Brownlow, filling the cafeteria.

"Boys and girls. Please be quiet for a moment." She

waited for quiet and continued. "Will Alyssa Reed come to the principal's office? Come to the principal's office immediately, Alyssa Reed."

"I hope everything's okay," Eloise said.

Blister picked up her lunch and dropped it in the trash.

"Good luck," Monster Bar called out.

She walked past Jakob's table without looking, facing straight ahead and hoping she wouldn't cry.

Everyone knew that the principal's message had something to do with trouble. Ms. Brownlow didn't come on the loudspeaker unless it was urgent.

Two policemen were sitting on the couch in the principal's office.

"You may or may not know that Jonah Morrison is missing," Ms. Brownlow said, indicating a chair to Blister.

"I do know."

"The officers have come to speak to students who are particularly friendly with Jonah and your name came up first."

The officers introduced themselves.

"Jonah was reported missing on Saturday afternoon by his mother. He went to bed and left sometime after breakfast."

"Ms. Morrison told me," Blister said.

"We just got your name from Ms. Morrison and tried to reach you yesterday, but your number was no longer in use."

"We moved to a new house and the telephone was just installed."

"Do you have any idea where he might be?" the officer asked.

Blister took a deep breath.

On the long walk from the lunchroom to the principal's office, she had made a decision. It wasn't even a decision, more like an inevitable conclusion that she had no choice if the police asked her if she knew what had happened.

"I know where he is," she said.

The officers and Ms. Brownlow and Blister walked the two blocks to Bixley Elementary.

They walked up the main steps of Bixley and stopped in the principal's office. The police and Ms. Brownlow spoke to Mr. Vagrant, the Bixley principal, who joined them on the walk to the assembly room.

Blister led the way, walking down the aisle, wondering what Jonah might be thinking. Of course he heard them coming and he knew it was Monday and there was no assembly. Maybe he could even see them and if he could, the first person he would see was Blister.

This would be the end of her friendship with Jonah. He would never forgive her for telling.

She walked up the steps to the stage, pulled back the curtains, and walked across the stage, stepping off the back of it.

"Under there," she said, pointing to the space under the stage.

The two policemen bent down and went ahead. Blister stood behind the stage with Ms. Brownlow and Mr. Vagrant. She could hear the policemen speaking to Jonah in their low voices, and she could hear Jonah's voice.

"I'd like to go now," she said to Ms. Brownlow. "I'd like to leave before he comes out."

Ms. Brownlow was thoughtful.

"Are you worried that he'll be angry at you?" she asked after a moment.

"I told on him," Blister said. "He won't want to see me."

"I think you should wait," Ms. Brownlow said. "You realize you have known where he was all along and didn't tell an adult, including his mother."

Blister's hands were wet, her mouth was dry, and she wanted to go home.

When the officers came out from under the stage, Jonah kept his head forward and walked between them.

"We can go now, Alyssa," Ms. Brownlow said. "Back to my office."

"Jonah didn't shoplift," Blister said. "I'd like to tell that to the police."

"Were you there when the shoplifting took place?"

"No, I wasn't."

"Then you don't have anything to say, do you?"

"I do."

"Nothing factual. You weren't a witness."

Blister walked the rest of the way in silence, following

Ms. Brownlow back to Memorial Junior High, up the steps, and along the corridor to her office.

"What do I do now?" she asked.

"You go to your afternoon classes and come to my office at the end of the school day," Ms. Brownlow said.

Jakob Cutter was at the far end of the basketball court with Eddie James and Monster Bar shooting hoops when Blister left the office and went out on the blacktop.

Jakob spotted her and headed over.

"Hey," he said, coming up to her, his breath smelling of licorice even in the cool October air. "Word's gotten around."

"What word?"

"That the police came to talk to you."

She sat down on the cool ground, too tired to stand, and drew her legs up under her chin.

"So what did the police ask you?" He leaned against a scraggly tree on the edge of the blacktop and put his hands in his pockets.

"The police asked me if I knew where Jonah was."

"Yeah?" He sat down beside her. "And you didn't."

Blister wrapped her arms tight around her knees.

"I did."

Jakob gave a long whistle. "Thumbs-up. So you knew all along?"

"Not all along. I guessed."

"So what did you tell the police?"

"I took them to the place where he was hiding."

"Jeez, Blister. I better watch out for you if I'm ever in trouble. Do you always tell on your friends?"

"Jonah will hate me."

"I guess he will."

Jakob leaned back on his elbows.

"Why didn't you lie?"

"I don't know why. I just couldn't."

"So that's the kind of girl you are?"

"They asked me if I knew where he was and I told the truth. There wasn't a plan to it."

Blister was aware of holding herself together, sitting very straight, her eyes forward, her body contained in case it would spill out on the blacktop if she moved too quickly.

On the hill above them, Monster Bar was making catcalls.

"Hey-y-y Jakob. Soft on redheads!"

Blister wrapped her arms around her knees.

"I'd like to know the truth about Friday night at the bus station."

"I don't know the truth," Jakob said. "I'm innocent."

"But you were there."

"Some of the time I was there and some of the time I wasn't and it just fell out that I wasn't there when something happened."

"I think you were there enough of the time to know."

"I was." Jakob was quiet, pulling at clumps of damp grass, rubbing them through his hands, wiping his hands on his baggy pants.

"I told Ms. Brownlow that Jonah hadn't shoplifted and she said I couldn't know whether or not he had because I wasn't a witness to what happened."

"Fair enough," Jakob said.

"So?"

Eloise and Annie and Vicky Sant came up the hill with ice-cream cones and Eloise let out a high screech.

"Blister and Jakob Cutter."

"Making time!" Monster Bar shouted.

"Making out," Eddie James called after him.

"K-I-S-S-I-N-G."

"I hate junior high," Blister said.

A wind picked up, lifting Blister's hair and blowing cool air across them. She stretched her fingers in the sun to warm them.

"So you want to know the truth of what happened on Friday night?"

Blister didn't look at him, didn't want to disturb the air between them, in case, just *in case* he had something genuine to tell her.

"So Friday night, as usual, I went to the bus station with Eddie and Monster Bar," be began quietly. "And Jonah followed us in that red flannel shirt he wears to cover the fat and his oversize empty backpack. We got there about eight o'clock and it was dark, but the electronics store was still open since it was a Friday night."

"Did you ask Jonah to go with you?"

"He just follows us around. Hard to shake him. It drives us crazy."

"So he was just hanging out with you at the bus station?"

"Not even. As soon as we knew he was following us like he does on Friday nights, every Friday night since the first week of school, we made a plan. We'd never had a plan before."

Jakob looked straight ahead, speaking deliberately.

"So I'm standing on the sidewalk and Jonah's leaning against the wall trying to look cool and his eyes are on Monster Bar. He's afraid of Monster Bar."

"And then what?"

"Jonah's backpack is beside him on the ground and he's watching Monster Bar, who has been given the job of distracting Jonah so he won't notice what I'm doing. I take the backpack and Jonah doesn't even notice. I swing into the electronics store like I'm looking for a friend, pick up a few things in the store, cell phones, CD players, iPods, a BlackBerry. I know how to get out the door without setting off the alarm so I do that and then there's a delay and the alarm goes off, but I'm already outside and have dropped the loaded backpack next to Jonah."

"And he didn't even notice?"

"He was in dreamland. He wouldn't notice a terrorist explosion."

Monster Bar came down the hill, jumped over Jakob, and fell facedown on the ground.

"Hello, citizens," he said, turning right side up. "So you're Jakob's girlfriend, right? Blister, the hot potato, right?"

Jakob was lying down on the grass, resting his head on his arm.

"I'm not his girlfriend," Blister said, grateful for the clanging of the fifth-period bell.

"So who're you with then if you're not with Jakob?" Monster Bar asked. "Jonah Morrison?"

"I don't have a boyfriend," Blister said, getting up, brushing the dirt off her pants. She slipped her backpack over her shoulder and headed down the hill.

Behind her, Jakob Cutter went back to shooting baskets with his friends, Jakob dribbling across the court, Eddie James running along beside him trying to wrest the basketball away.

Blister stopped at the top step of the back entrance to Memorial and watched them, amazed at what Jakob Cutter had said.

He didn't have to tell her anything. He could easily have lied.

15

Heads or Tails?

by the time Blister got to homeroom, it was only one-thirty, two more hours to the end of classes and then a meeting with Ms. Brownlow.

"I need to go home," she said to Ms. Newton before the bell rang for sixth period.

"You have a reason?"

"Strep throat," Blister said.

Ms. Newton raised her eyebrows and sent her to the nurse.

The nurse took her temperature, which was normal. Then she looked at her throat, which showed no evidence of infection, and told her to go back to class.

"I won't," Blister said, winding her spaghetti legs around each other, wrapping her arms tight across her chest.

"You WON'T go back to class?" the nurse asked.

If she'd decided on the stomach flu, she would have been sent home without a question. There was no way to prove she had not thrown up in the girls' room. Strep throat was a mistake.

"Is WON'T what I heard you say?" The nurse was standing over her, a thermometer in one hand, the other hand on her hip. She was a big woman, not unattractive, but at that moment she seemed to have the size to flatten Blister on the floor of the infirmary.

"I'm having a nervous breakdown." Blister's words were measured.

"A nervous breakdown is not an illness," the nurse said coolly. "Describe your illness. I can't call your mother unless you describe what's going on."

She leaned in so close, Blister felt the heat of her body on her own skin.

"Trouble at school?" the large nurse asked. "Trouble at home?"

"Never mind. I have no trouble at all," Blister said, walking out of the infirmary to her locker.

She wrote a note to Ms. Brownlow to say that she was

going home for the day and wouldn't be checking in with her until the following morning, gave the note to the receptionist, and went out of the front door of Memorial Junior High. At the end of the building was a public telephone and she called her mother.

Mary Reed was at her job at the flower shop in the next town, so she asked Daisy G. to pick up Blister and take her to the doctor.

"I'm sick in the heart," Blister said, climbing into the car. "I don't need the doctor."

"Heartsick is the worst," Daisy G. said.

Blister fastened her seat belt, slid down in the front seat, and put her feet on the dashboard.

She had acquired a new unspoken reserve — "Don't bother me," it said. She put her hands over her eyes to close out the sun. She had never known such tiredness, as if her blood and muscles had drained into the ground and what was left of her, loose around her skeleton, was empty skin.

Daisy G. pulled into the parking lot of Fresh Organic and opened the car door.

"Come with me, chicken soup," she said. "I need to get the groceries for dinner."

"I'm staying here," she said.

"Because you're feeling sick?"

"Because I don't want to go to the grocery store."

She wasn't ready to tell Daisy G. about Jonah. Everyone would know soon enough. And she didn't want Jakob's story to slip away into the hands of the grown-ups until she had decided what she was going to do.

Grown-ups had a way of taking over, of making a bad situation worse.

Daisy G. took her purse and slid the keys into her pocket.

"Chicken marsala for dinner or chicken cacciatore?"

"Chicken marsala," Blister said.

She slid down in her seat, burrowing her face in her knees, closing her eyes to keep out the sun.

An image of Jonah in the supply closet at Bixley came swimming up. There was a slender shaft of light and she saw him squished into a corner behind the paper towels and lemonade, watching her with an expression of such sweetness on his face.

She couldn't remember whether this moment had actually happened or if she had invented it to compensate for her betrayal of him with the police.

But Jonah Morrison had felt something for her that she had never experienced from another person.

Maybe that was love.

"Puppy love," Daisy G. would say.

But whatever it was coming from Jonah was new and fragile to her and she felt as if she could break him.

She didn't know what to expect now or whether they would ever be friends again.

Daisy G. opened the car door.

"Fresh blueberries from California, French vanilla ice cream, chicken for marsala, superfine sugar, and I've decided to add a little color on the top of the Strawberry Surprise," Daisy G. said, loading her groceries in the backseat, hopping in the front. "Blueberries and kiwi and some whole strawberries on a puff of whipped cream. Yum?"

Tears were rising behind Blister's eyes and she pressed her palms against her face to stop them.

Daisy G. ran her fingers through Blister's bristly hair.

"Whatever is the matter, buttercup, we'll fix it quickly, as soon as we get home."

They drove down Main, past Bixley, around the corner, and down the avenue, turning off just before Memorial Junior High, where classes were letting out.

When they got home, Frank was in the kitchen talking on the phone. Blister walked straight upstairs, picked up Bewilder on the landing, and locked the door to her bedroom.

For a long time, she sat at her desk on edge, waiting to see what would happen next, certain that something would . . . and soon. Someone would call or knock on the front door. Maybe it would be the police to say that Jonah was at the police precinct, or Jakob Cutter would arrive with flowers or a candy bar or something from the variety store wrapped in shiny paper as payment to her for not telling on him. Or maybe Ms. Morrison would call with bad news.

She was sick with worry about Jonah. She didn't even have room in her crowded brain to consider what to do with

Jakob's confession. She was not surprised by what he had told her since she had already imagined the events of Friday night. But she was astonished that he'd told her at all.

Jakob Cutter came first. He stood at the front door in his old blue jean jacket and a baseball cap.

"I gotta see you," he said to Blister. "Out here on the porch."

"Can't you come inside?" Blister said.

He checked around the porch.

"I'm watching out for Monster Bar, who's coming over."

He looked down the street.

"Have you told anyone what I told you today?"

Blister hesitated. She hadn't made up her mind yet what to do.

"I've got to know."

"I haven't told anyone."

"Is that the truth?"

"It's the truth so far," she said.

Up the street, Monster Bar in his baseball cap was running toward them.

"I'll probably end up in one of those detention homes, right?" Jakob said.

"I don't know," Blister said. "I don't know anything about detention homes."

"I'll let you know how the food is," Jakob said. "But thanks for not ratting on me so far."

And he jumped down the front steps, meeting Monster Bar in the street.

Back inside the house, she could see Jakob through the bay window in the living room, standing on the sidewalk with Monster Bar, who was laughing.

She picked up the telephone and dialed Jonah, who answered at the first ring.

"Morrison residence," he said.

"It's me," she said.

There was a hesitation, his breath thick as pudding in the receiver, and in the background she heard Quentin demanding TV.

"Jonah?" she said.

And he hung up.

* * *

"BLISTER!"

She heard her name and looked out the window. Eddie James had arrived and the three of them were lined up, sitting on the porch. Monster Bar headed across the street, ran up to her front porch, and called again.

"BLISTER!"

She opened the front door.

"Hey Blister, come on over," Monster Bar said, walking back across the street. "How's tricks?" he called.

"Tricky," Eddie James said, falling off the top step laughing. "Very tricky. Gotta watch out for little Miss Blister Reed, don'tcha know. She could land you in the slammer."

"Does everybody know what happened?" Blister asked Jakob, crossing the street.

"Everybody on this front porch knows everything."

Monster Bar blew air in her direction.

"Shut up, Monster Bar," Jakob said. "That's not what she's asking."

"What's she asking then?" Eddie James said. "For a Christmas present from us?"

"She's asking if you guys know that I told her what happened Friday night."

"Yeah, we know," Monster Bar said.

"We're not worried about it, if that's what you're wondering," Eddie James said. "Like, big deal."

"Does that mean you're telling no one?" Monster Bar said.

"It means nothing. She doesn't know what she's going to do with the info yet."

"Are you kidding?" Eddie James stood up, clenching his fists.

"I got a plan, Jakob. Let's stuff her in your duffel and drown her in the river," Monster Bar said.

"Leave her alone." Jakob pressed down on Eddie James's shoulder. "What happened Friday night is not a secret any longer. Got it?"

"So we'll drown *you*, comrade," Monster Bar said.

"Be my guest," Jakob replied.

Blister turned quickly, wanting to get away from the conversation, and headed across Acorn Street to her house.

Frank was at the front door when she came in.

"Ms. Morrison called," he said. "I know what's happened. At least I know some of what's happened."

She followed him to the kitchen and sat down at the table, where Daisy G. was slathering whipped cream on the Strawberry Surprise.

"Which part of what happened do you know?" Blister asked.

"I know you found Jonah at Bixley on Saturday. I know you told the police today where he was. I assume you were trying to protect Jonah and when the police came, you couldn't protect him any longer."

"But I lied to you," Blister said.

"You were protecting Jonah."

"He would have killed me if I'd told. He still will."

"Ms. Morrison called to say that Jonah and the other boys were meeting at the police station with their parents at seven o'clock and asked for us to be there," Frank Holt said.

"Oh great," Blister said, and she headed upstairs to change.

16

One Kind of Truth

frank Holt parked the truck in the lot of the second precinct next to a red Cherokee Jeep that Blister had seen in the driveway of the Cutters' house.

"I'm staying in the truck," Daisy G. said, sitting in the backseat next to Blister with the Strawberry Surprise in a Pyrex dish on her lap.

"If things go well with the police, we'll have a celebration." Daisy G. stuck her finger along the side of the cake and licked the whipped icing. "You never know."

A black SUV drove up and Monster Bar got out, walking in front of his father, who was short and squat with greased hair that stood out from his forehead like a shelf. Monster Bar gave Blister a withering look.

"Friend?" Frank asked her.

"Enemy," Blister said. "That's Monster Bar."

"Do you think Jonah is here yet?" Mary Reed asked, but Blister didn't answer. "Well, that boy across the street is here."

"Jakob Cutter," Frank Holt said.

Through the glass window of the police station, Blister saw Jonah sitting next to Ms. Morrison, who was holding Quentin, in the process of a temper tantrum, on her lap. Jonah was staring straight ahead, his hands in the pockets of his jacket, his head up. He looked at Blister straight in the eye as if he had never seen her before.

Jakob was dressed in good clothes, a cotton shirt with a collar and khakis, and nodded at Blister when she came in. His mother, the baby over her shoulder, waved to Mary Reed and Frank.

Two officers came out and led the families into a large room with a table and chairs. Eddie James was already sitting there, his head in his hands, without his parents.

"My parents are in Alaska," he said when the police came in.

"Who's taking care of you?" one of the policemen asked.

"I'm taking care of myself."

"Your parents know you're here?" the policeman asked.

"I don't think so," Eddie James said. "Unless my grandmother told them."

"Your grandmother's home?"

Eddie nodded.

"Call her," the officer said. "She's going to have to be here if she's the adult in charge of you while your parents are away."

He handed a phone to Eddie.

The policeman indicated that everyone should take a seat around the table.

"This is outrageous," Monster Bar's father said, walking into the room behind Frank Reed, taking a seat at the end of the table. "You got a kid with stolen merchandise in his backpack and there's a question who stole the merchandise? Give me a break."

Jonah sat across from Blister, looking just beyond her so they couldn't make eye contact.

"I'm Officer Blanco and this is Officer Adams," the older policeman said. "We're specialized juvenile

210

detectives and we'll be speaking to each of you individually, so I'd like you to introduce yourselves."

"Alyssa Reed," Blister said, high spirits filling her voice again. She was feeling herself, her heart thumping in her chest so she could almost hear it, her blood rushing through her veins as if at any moment bolts of electricity would send her like a firecracker into the air. "I'm Jonah Morrison's best friend."

"Mary Reed."

"Frank Holt. I'm here for Alyssa."

The officer turned to Jakob.

"Sandra Cutter. I'm Jakob's mother."

"Jakob Cutter."

"Eddie James," Eddie said, swallowing the words so the officer asked him to speak up and then speak up again.

"Monster Bar."

"Do you have another name?" the officer asked.

"William."

"Bar?"

"Yeah, William Bar, but nobody calls me that."

"My name's William Bar, the first," his father said.

"Ms. Alelia Morrison and this is my son, Jonah."

"I am Jonah Morrison," Jonah said clearly.

"On Friday night, our officers were alerted that there'd been a robbery at Ram's Electronics and two officers reported immediately to the shop downtown next to the bus station. Outside the store, they found Jonah Morrison with a backpack full of electronic equipment. When they asked him if the backpack was his, he said it was. When they asked where he'd gotten the electronic equipment, he said he didn't know how it had gotten into his backpack. His backpack had been empty when he came to the bus station. He was charged with shoplifting, which he denied, and the officers brought him to the precinct, where his mother picked him up. Since then we have been on the case and spoken to a couple of you. We've asked all of you to come because you were at the bus station with Jonah."

"How come you asked Blister to come? She wasn't at the bus station," Jakob said.

Officer Blanco looked confused.

"Alyssa. Blister is my alias."

"She has been helping us."

"Right, a lot of help you get from Blister," Monster Bar said.

"How long is this going to take?" Eddie James asked. "I've got homework."

Jakob and Monster Bar exchanged glances. Eddie James hadn't done his homework since second grade.

"It's going to take a while," Officer Blanco said. "We're not getting started with *you* until your grandmother gets here."

Across the table, Blister could hear puffs of Jonah's irregular breathing and guessed that he was holding in his tears.

Monster Bar went first, following the officers down a corridor with his father, disappearing behind a door.

Eddie James's grandmother arrived shortly after Monster Bar left with the police.

"I was in my nightgown watching TV," she said, hurrying into the room wearing her Wellington boots and a long raincoat although the weather was fine. "What now, Eddie?"

Eddie shrugged.

"These guys and me were at a place where a shoplifting happened." He pointed to Jonah. "He did the shoplifting, but they asked us to come here as witnesses even though we didn't witness anything since the shoplifting happened after we had left. Right, Jakob?"

Jakob nodded.

"Jakob's one of the guys I hang out with," Eddie said. "This is my grandmother."

"I'm Mrs. James." She introduced herself around the table. "Well, I'll tell you this, Eddie David James. I'm counting the minutes until your parents get home from their vacation."

She took a seat next to Jonah, took off her coat, and leaned over to Jonah.

"You just don't look like the kind of boy who gets into trouble. But then, what do I know?"

"We were standing there by the bus station eating chocolate-covered cherries, which I got at the drugstore, and then we had an idea of going someplace else and we left Jonah, who isn't exactly our friend, standing by the electronics store," Eddie James said. "At least that's the way I remember it, right, Jakob?"

Jakob didn't reply. He sat with his hands folded on the table in front of him and didn't take his eyes off the window across from him, which faced the back parking lot of the police station.

Monster Bar came down the corridor, followed by his father and Officer Blanco.

"Okay," he said to the officer. "Thanks a lot. Me and my dad have got to be headed home."

"Not yet," Officer Blanco said. "We finish talking to everyone and then we assemble here and I say something to you as a group and then you leave. Not soon. Maybe a couple more hours."

"Yeah?" Monster Bar folded his arms across his chest.

"Take a seat," the officer said. "We'll be back in a minute."

"What're you going to do, talk about me behind my back?" Monster Bar asked.

"Hush," Monster Bar's father said. "Don't be stupid."

The officers walked down the corridor without responding.

"So that was easy," Monster Bar said. "A few questions and I'm out of there. I thought it was going to be bad, but it isn't so bad."

Blister was watching Jonah under her half-closed lids so he wouldn't notice she was looking at him. Ms. Morrison's hand was lightly on his arm, but Jonah didn't move, didn't change his expression even when Quentin pulled at his hair.

She knew what she was going to do. She just didn't know when.

Once, her mother leaned over and whispered, asking her what she planned to say.

"I don't know the questions," Blister said, and Monster Bar overheard her.

"One thing about you, Blister, is that you weren't at the bus station so you can't be a reliable witness."

"I don't think we should be having these conversations while we're sitting here in the police precinct waiting to be questioned by the juvenile detectives," Ms. Morrison said.

Frank Holt agreed. He had a big voice and people listened when he used it. The room fell silent.

Eddie James was the next to go and his grandmother followed him, carrying her raincoat.

"High five," Monster Bar said as Eddie walked by, but Eddie didn't respond.

"I'm next," Jakob said.

Blister noticed he was leaning against his mother, not in an exaggerated way, but his body was at an angle and his shoulder poked into hers. He looked frightened and she felt a rush of sympathy for him.

And then she caught his attention. He looked away quickly, but he had registered her intentions.

"Please don't forget what you told me," she said when Jakob and his mother were called back with the officers.

Monster Bar gave her a terrible look.

"What was that?" Frank Holt whispered.

Blister shook her head.

Jakob was gone for a very long time. Monster Bar must have gotten nervous because he walked back and forth along the table, muttering swear words under his breath. When Eddie James and his grandmother came back, she was irritated at Eddie for making her miss her favorite TV show.

It was almost ten o'clock when the officers came out alone, without Jakob, to tell the Reeds and the Morrisons that they could leave now. They shook hands with Jonah and told him next time he hung out at the bus station he ought to keep his backpack over his shoulder and pay attention to what was going on.

"How come we can leave?" Jonah asked, perplexed, as he often was with the way things went.

"Jakob has confessed to shoplifting and filling your backpack with the merchandise."

"What about us?" Monster Bar said, red in the face. "Eddie and me?"

"We want you to stay. You were there when it happened."

Blister sat next to Jonah on a bench outside the police station.

"I'd like to wait until Jakob comes out so I can thank him for telling the truth," she said to Frank and her mother.

"I'd like to thank him too," Jonah said. He turned to Blister. "That was amazing, wasn't it?"

"That he told the truth?"

"Pretty amazing." His face was flushed and his breath thin. "Are you going to be his girlfriend now?"

Blister shook her head.

"Do you think he'll go to a juvenile detention home?"

"Frank said he'll be put on some kind of probation when he appears before the judge, but he won't have to go to a juvenile detention home."

"Good," Jonah said.

"I'm glad," Blister said. "Daisy G. made you a celebration cake just in case."

"In case you're going to be my girlfriend?"

"I hated the way you were with me at school, Jonah."

"I hated watching you and Jakob Cutter sitting on the Bixley steps together."

"But it wasn't true what you thought," Blister said. "Jakob is Jakob. I thought I knew exactly who he was and I was wrong."

"What are you telling me? That you won't be my girlfriend because Jakob turned out to be good?" Jonah asked.

"It has nothing to do with Jakob, but he did turn out to be different than I thought."

Blister took a deep breath and leaned against the bench. She knew what she wanted to say, but she couldn't find the words to say it. That was the trouble with words.

"You're my best friend, Jonah," she said quietly. "That's what you are forever."

"Best friend. What's that?" Jonah asked. "It's not enough."

"It's everything," Blister said. "I've never had a friend like you."

She stretched, watching her mother leaning against Frank Holt.

Jakob Cutter had surprised her. She didn't imagine that he would tell the truth first to her and then to the police. Like Frank Holt had surprised her with his sweetness. But mostly, she had surprised herself. All weekend she had been riding up and down on a seesaw of emotions and then, almost as if she hadn't seen it coming, the seesaw balanced exactly in the familiar middle.

"What do you mean by forever?" Jonah asked.

"Just this, you and me sitting next to each other, on and on and on," Blister said, leaning her shoulder against Jonah with just enough pressure that he didn't lose his balance and fall off the bench.

Jonah wasn't exactly happy, but he would be, she thought, soon, maybe even tonight.